DAMAGED 2
A Novel

By

H.M. Ward

www.SexyAwesomeBooks.com

Laree Bailey Press

CHAPTER 1

After Sam leaves, Peter picks up his cell phone. His gaze lifts and meets mine. It's like his heart is caught in his throat. He's thinking something, but I don't know what. Those sapphire eyes lower when Peter looks at the phone cradled in his hand. "Let's take our time getting out of here and put some space between you and Dean. I need to make a call and then we can sort out the details. Okay?" When he finally looks up, I get the feeling that Peter isn't telling me something.

"Who are you calling?"

"My brother. I need to ask him something." Peter turns abruptly with determination across his face. His features harden and he no longer looks like the man I know.

I don't snoop and linger at the door listening to that phone call. There's something between him and his brother, old scars maybe. I don't want to make Peter's life harder. Maybe I should go? I mean, this isn't his fight. It's mine. Just because I utterly failed last time doesn't mean that I'll get the crap beat out of me this time. I glance at my hands, which are covered in scabs. Damn it. I don't know what to do. I glance back at Peter's room.

The decision is taken from me when his door opens and Peter walks out. Tension lines his neck and shoulders. His jaw shifts from side to side as though the conversation he just had pissed him off. His eyes flick up from the floor and meet mine. "My brother's an asshole."

I smile at him. "So is mine."

Peter watches me for a moment and sighs. He runs his hands through his hair and stretches. The anger that was there washes away, but it's not totally gone. "I need to tell you something." The way he says it makes my stomach dip. The tone, the way he looks away from me sends a shiver down my spine. The words hang in the air like a bad omen.

Peter takes my hands and pulls me over to the couch. At first we're seated next to each other and he's holding my hand, but it's like he can't sit still. Peter is on his feet moments later, pacing. Every few seconds he tries to tell me something but can't choose the right words. Peter makes an aggravated sound in the back of his throat as he works his jaw. When he turns and looks at me, I know there's something wrong.

Peter's lips are parted as he stares at me. "I didn't want to bring this up, not now, but you need to know something about me." He swallows hard and looks away.

I push off the couch and walk over to him. "You can tell me anything." When I touch his arm, Peter flinches. The movement is so subtle but speaks volumes. It makes me nervous. Why is he acting this way? I kid to try to lighten his mood. "You're not the one who put the squirrel outside the bathroom window, are you?"

Peter snorts a surprised laugh and looks over at me. He takes me in his arms and pulls me to his chest. It feels so good, so safe. He kisses the top of my head. "Do you know anything about the Ferro family?"

His question confuses me, but I nod. "Yeah, who doesn't?"

"Tell me what you know." I step back and look into his face, but it doesn't clarify anything.

Oh-kay? This seems like a weird question, but I answer him anyway. "Well, they have more cash in their pockets than Scrooge has in his money bin. The mom is a hard-ass, the dad is a player with a new mistress every other week, and the three sons can't seem to stay out of trouble.

"The youngest, Jonathan, was in the paper the other day for doing something stupid, but most people forget that and get blindsided by his charm—and his looks. The oldest brother, Sean, is estranged; at least that's what the paper said. Same thing goes for the middle child." I have no idea where he's going with this. I stop talking and wait for him to clue me in, but he doesn't.

"What else have you heard?"

"Nothing really. The same stuff you heard, probably."

"I doubt it, but go on."

I give him a weird look and think back. "The oldest brother was accused of killing his wife. He was in the news for a long time until he got off. After that, Sean left the family and walked away from all that money. The papers started calling it the curse of the Ferro fortune or something like that. After the oldest brother left, the next heir was Pete Ferro. A few weeks later he was proposing to his fiancée in Rockefeller Center and..." I stop talking. My eyes go wide.

Peter's grip on my hands tightens. "Say it. Finish the story, Sidney."

Swallowing hard, I continue because it can't be, no matter how striking the similarities. "And she was killed. Pete was stabbed in the side. He seemed to drift for a while, not taking an interest in anything, until one day he disappeared. He walked away from the Ferro fortune completely."

As our eyes lock I realize that this is his story. My jaw quivers and I don't know what to think. Part of me wants to yell at him for not telling me that he's Peter Fucking Ferro, but the other part is afraid. The Ferro brothers have a reputation, and he's one of them. I stand there too long and blurt out, "You're Pete Ferro."

He's watching me; his blue eyes are locked on mine. Peter nods slowly. He rubs his thumb over the back of my hand. "Yeah, I am." I blink, too shocked to speak. "It's not something I talk about. It's part of my past, Sidney. When I lost Gina, I walked away from everything. Sean was gone and my parents aren't exactly helpful. My mother's solution to everything is to see a shrink. I tried that. I decided the best way to get on with my life was to start over, so I did. I took Gina's last name and finished my doctoral work." He shrugs like it isn't a big deal. "Then I came here and met you."

"You're Sean Ferro's brother?" He nods. It feels like I'm lost in a dream, being sucked in deeper and deeper. "How? How could you...?" I falter. I don't know what to say. I can't say what's racing through my mind. How could you help cover up a murder? How could you be related to someone like that? How could you be the Pete Ferro, the player, who is so much like his father?

People said Peter didn't love Gina, that it was a marriage/business merger, but that's not true. Peter did love her. I hear it in his voice. That night haunts him.

"I'm sorry I didn't tell you before now. I didn't want them to find me. I wanted a chance to start over. You can understand that."

"That's not the same. What I did is not the same! I ran from someone who was hurting me. How could you help him?" *How could you help your brother cover up brutalizing his wife?* The question is lodged in my throat. I can't spit it out because it strikes too close to home. Something snaps inside my mind. I feel duped, like he tricked me. The public perception of Peter is nothing like the man I've fallen in love with. One of them is fake, but I don't know which one. It makes my heart race, and I'm scared that I've lost him, that Peter was never really mine—that my Peter doesn't exist.

I rip my hands out of his grip and start backing away. The look on his face isn't comforting. Peter doesn't correct me, which makes it worse. "Who are you? Do I know you at all?"

"Sidney, you know me—"

"Then why does it feel like I don't? Why does it feel like you've been lying to me this whole time?" Tears make my eyes sting, but I don't let them fall. "I have to think. I have to go."

Peter darts in front of me and blocks the door. "I can't let you leave. Not with Dean out there waiting for you."

"Am I really safer in here?"

Peter flinches as if I slapped him. He steps away from the door and opens it. "You know who I am better than anyone else. Names don't matter, not to me. If you think I've misled you on everything and that I've been lying to you since the beginning, then walk through that door and don't come back." His gaze narrows as he waits for me to decide.

I don't know what to think, and I can't believe he said that to me. I'm speaking without realizing what I'm saying. It's all gut instinct, and right now my guts feel like they've been spinning in a Gravitron for twenty years. "Names mean something, Peter, or you wouldn't have hidden yours from me. You're not the man I thought you were. I can't even—" I shake my head and push past him.

I walk out the door and fly down the staircase. I don't stop. Peter calls after me from the landing above. I jump into the car and peel out of the parking lot as fast as I can. I need to think, but I can't. Everything I know about Peter Ferro is crashing into everything I know about Peter Granz. Nothing fits—there's no thread, no continuity. My mind reels, searching for a thread—anything—when it snags on something Peter did. At the time I thought it was good, but it cinches Peter to his past, binding them together. It's the whispered threats to Sam and the way my brother went white as a sheet. The things the Ferro family can do, have done, makes my tears turn to big, ugly sobs.

I pull into a parking lot and slam my hands on the steering wheel. Another liar. Another man who made me think he's one person and then turns out to be someone else. It feels like my heart has been ripped out of my chest. I can't breathe. I tip my head back and scream. If Peter said any other family name, I'd be stupid for walking away—but he said Ferro. That family is so messed up. It doesn't make me feel sorry for Peter; it makes me feel played. He used me. Peter wove a web of lies and I laid down in the center.

Peter's been lying to everyone about everything. I wonder if Strictland knows who he really is, if she caught it when she hired him. I would have never put them together. The Pete Ferro I remember from the countless sightings was surly, rude, and nothing like the man I've spent the past three months with.

I'm done with this, done with him. I can't take the heartache.

I can't.

I won't.

CHAPTER 2

When I pull up in front of the dorm, Millie is standing there with my suitcase already packed. She steps toward the car when I roll to a stop. After tossing my bag in the backseat, she says, "Are you sure you want to drive up there all by yourself?" Concern covers her face. I nod. I don't trust myself to talk. "I can come with you. I just have to finish up my term paper and we can go. Or I can come now and ask the prof for an extension. You shouldn't take off by yourself, not with your mom sick."

"I've driven it alone before. I'll be fine, Millie. Finish up the semester and have fun with Brent."

Millie's mouth is open, but she doesn't say anything else. When she changes the topic, I feel blindsided. "Where's Dr. Granz?"

"I don't care." My grip tightens on the steering wheel.

"What should I tell him when he comes looking for you?"

I glance at her, suspicious. "When he comes looking? What makes you think he's coming?"

"Brent was with a group of guys on the Intramural Field last night. He said something happened, that Dr. Granz was there. The university said he broke up a fight." She swallows hard. "Rumor has it that you were the reason they were fighting."

I grab my head with my hands and close my eyes. I pinch out all the light, the dorm, the noise, and try to let it roll off. Of course people would think that. Everyone thought I was screwing my teacher all year. *Fine. Whatever.*

"Sidney—" Millie starts.

I cut her off and take her hands through the window. It's a normal gesture, something I do to keep Millie focused when I'm telling her something important. I don't even think about it. "It wasn't like that, okay? Believe whatever you want, but it wasn't—" The words dry up in my throat when Millie takes my wrists and turns my palms over.

Her eyes have that knowing look when her gaze meets mine. "Sidney, what happened? It looks like you tried to claw your way through a brick wall."

I snatch my hands back and push my hair out of my face. "Nothing." My jaw locks. I want to leave. I don't want to talk about it. I don't want to tell her anything. There's no single explanation. One answer makes twenty more questions, and I don't want her to know what Dean did to me.

"That's not nothing."

"I fell, okay? Last night when I came out of English, I fell."

"Then what about Granz? People are saying he—"

"Millie." I cut her off. "I have to go. I'll call you and fill you in, okay?"

She nods, which makes her blonde curls bob back and forth. "Fine, but I think you're being stupid." She leaves it open-ended, as if I'm stupid for so many things.

"I'll miss you, too. See you in time for Summer Session, okay?" Millie nods and steps away from the car. We are supposed to take a class on feminism together this summer. I begged her to take it with me, which means if I'm not back with my butt in a chair in twenty-two days, Millie will kill me.

"You better. Otherwise I'll turn into a feminazi and you'll be my bitch." She winks at me in a distinctly southern way, which takes the bite out of her words.

It makes me laugh. "I will. I'll call you once I get going."

"Fine, but don't text me while you're driving seventy-five miles per hour. I don't want to tell everyone in my eulogy that you act really stupid sometimes. And, Sidney…"

I resist the urge to roll my eyes. "Yeah?"

"No matter what's happening with you, I'll always have your back. You know that, right?"

Aw crap. Millie gives me big, fat doe eyes. Between my hands, my mood, and the rumors about Peter, she knows something's going on. "Fine," I grumble. "Get in, but if you ask to pee every five seconds, I'll leave you on the side of the road." Millie squees and bounces into the seat. "Don't you need clothes?"

"Psh." She waves a hand at me and grins. "They're already in your suitcase. You seriously think that I'd make you do this by yourself? Get real." Millie pulls her seat belt across her lap as she scolds me.

"Nice nineties verbiage."

"Suck it."

We both start laughing as I pull away. I'm so emotionally fried and really want to be alone, but Millie's right—I shouldn't try to do this on my own. Maybe it will help to have her along.

It's strange—at one time this little town was my refuge, but now it's strangling me. I want to put distance between me and Peter as fast as possible. My stomach twists thinking about him. I can't believe he's a Ferro. I can't believe my life has gotten so messed up so fast. Seeing Dean was bad enough. I can't wait to hit the interstate and get the hell out of here.

CHAPTER 3

There's a long strip of nothing between the college and the next town. I'm lost in thought when Millie finally says, "So are you going to tell me what happened last night?"

I glance at her out of the corner of my eye. "I really don't want to talk about it."

"Okay, then tell me something else. What's up with you and Professor Hottie? I mean, I'd wanna get with that—"

"Oh my God!" I roll my eyes. I can't help it. Clutching the wheel tighter, I think fast. Maybe I should just tell her. That's better than talking about Peter. Damn him. I still can't believe he lied to me. I let out a huff of air. "Fine. Last night my ex-asshole-boyfriend showed up and tried to drag me away. I fell and the pavement didn't agree with my palms, okay?"

Her jaw is hanging open. "Fuck, no! Not okay. What boyfriend? Why'd he drag you across the parking lot?" She spews a ton of other questions at me until I cut her off.

"Dean. We dated back in high school. *Dated* is the wrong word." I swallow hard. My throat is so tight. Memories come rushing back, and it's all I can do to force them down and control my voice. "He raped me. I don't want to talk about it, but I thought you should know." Odds are Dean and Sam are following the same route out of Texas, unless they took a farm road, which is doubtful.

Millie's jaw is hanging open. Slowly, she closes it as her eyes get glassy, and she presses her palms into my arm. "Sidney, I had no idea…"

If she cries, I'll cry. I snap at her without meaning to. "Don't apologize. I hate it when people apologize. It doesn't change anything. That's why I never talk about it, okay?" She looks as if I slapped her with a board, sitting rigid in the seat, bobbing her head in a yes motion.

"I'm sorry, Millie. I just don't know what to do. Dean was everything. I thought he loved me. I don't know what happened. One minute things were fine, and then they weren't. It sounds stupid, but I wasn't even sure if it happened. Not until a few times later.

"When Dean found me last night, he was here with my brother. I told my family back before I came here, but they didn't believe me." I wonder if she believes me. It makes my jaw clamp shut and my words stop. I can't spill my guts to people who don't have faith in me. I can't trust them at all. Not after everything that happened. It feels like there's a sack of sand on my chest. I can barely breathe.

She gives me a sad smile and looks out the window. "I kind of know what you mean. It's not the same thing, but I dated a guy when I first got here. He wanted too much, too fast. I didn't want to keep going, but he wouldn't let me stop." She makes a face and I know she's remembering it.

"Uh, Millie. That is the same thing, unless you didn't tell him no."

"I told him no." She's quiet again.

I want to punch something. I can't believe this happened to her. All this time I thought I was alone. But I don't understand how she flirts and acts like it's nothing. My reaction makes me shut down and push people away. I want them at a safe distance. Millie is all smiles and giddy giggles. She acts like nothing bad ever happened to her. Holy crap, was I wrong. The urge to say *sorry* hits me, but I don't say it because I hate it when people say it to me. "Did you see him again?"

"No. He didn't think I was worth the effort."

"What an asshole. Did you report it?"

She gives me a weird look. "And say what? I was almost having sex with some guy when he decided to have sex with me? No, I didn't report it. It was my fault. I shouldn't have gone out with him in the first place. I led him on."

"Millie, are you serious? It's not your fault. How is it your fault?"

She smiles softly and glances at me out of the corner of her eye. "Are you seriously asking me that question? You know how it feels. Logic doesn't exactly take over, and it's easier to admit I made a mistake than to..." She shakes her head and looks out the window.

I'm quiet for a moment. Everything between Millie and me shifts in a matter of moments. She understands this in a way no one else does. "I know what you mean, but it's harder to admit to being overpowered like that. I used to think that women and men were equal in every way, right up until that started happening. My mom loves Dean and looked the other way. My whole family did. My brother thought I was just trying to get attention. This morning Sam seemed to actually wonder if I'd been telling the truth."

"What made him do that?"

"Peter. Peter did it. He has a way of saying things." Peter Ferro, not my beautiful Peter Granz. Peter Granz doesn't exist.

I feel Millie's gaze on the side of my face and look over at her. "You've got it so bad."

"What?" I squirm in my seat and laugh nervously. "I don't—"

"Deny it all you want, but you have a serious crush on Professor Peter. Mr. Swingdance. Mr. Sexybuns." She grins wickedly at me and makes a rude gesture.

"Millie! I can't believe you just did that!"

Millie laughs hysterically and leans into the door. "Dude, you realize that you have no gas, right?"

"I was going to get some when we got to Dallas."

"Well, I'm not pushing the car when we run out of gas. You better stop at the next exit. Besides, I want a snack. I'm starving. I skipped lunch to keep my lunatic roommate from driving cross-country by herself. She's so crazy. You have no idea."

"And you need to pee."

"And I might need to powder my nose. You're so crass, Sidney."

"I try."

I shake my head and pull off the interstate. There's not much between the college and Dallas except flat, dead land and scattered cattle. Mesquite trees jut up from the dry ground periodically with their branches looking like withered fingers. There aren't many places to stop, and my tank isn't full, so I decide Millie's right and pull off. Pushing the car in hundred-degree heat would suck.

We roll to a stop in front of a gas station that's a million years old. The pumps don't have credit card readers, so I have to go inside. "So much for pay at the pump," I mutter, and follow Millie toward the door.

She skips ahead of me and makes a beeline for the bathroom. The inside of the gas station is supposed to be rustic, but it just feels dirty to me. There are shelves of food and soda machines. An old clerk with a handlebar mustache is sitting behind the cash register. He doesn't seem to blink.

I wonder whether he's sleeping with his eyes open.

When I step toward the counter and lift my gaze, I look around quickly. There's a woman buying bread, and behind her, a row over, there is one other person in the store. Our eyes lock and we see each other at the same time. My heart pounds harder and faster as my stomach goes into a free fall.

In that moment, everything changes.

CHAPTER 4

Those green eyes used to haunt me every time I went to sleep. I feel my body stiffen. It remembers what Dean did to me with the slightest provocation. Dean flashes that smile at me, the one that's all swagger and charm. He walks around the aisle and comes toward me. I'm frozen in place. It's like last night all over again. The shock of seeing him when I'd never expect to throws me off. No one ever stops here. It's too close to town, but my brother and Dean wouldn't know that.

My pulse increases with each step he takes toward me. My fingers twitch at my sides as the muscles tense up, ready to fight. But Dean doesn't want a fight, not in a public place like this. There are too many people around. I doubt Dean will do anything. The man seems to turn into a monster only at night, although I'm sure if he could get me alone now he'd happily pick up where he left off.

Dean stops in front of me. "Hey, baby." He looks so goddamn normal. There's nothing plastered across his face that says otherwise. I wish there had been. I wish I'd known.

People can be two-faced like that. An image of Peter flashes behind my eyes. Screw them. I don't need anyone.

I come back to myself. Anger frees me, and the fear trickles away. "Don't baby me, and if you come a step closer—"

Dean gives me a lopsided grin and steps closer. "You'll what, Sidney? Come on. We both know you don't have it in you." He's a breath away from me. Dean slips his hand on my waist and leans in closer, whispering in my ear, "Just wait until we get home and I get you alone. I've learned some new tricks while you were away." When he backs off, I'm frozen in place. My body is covered in a sheet of icy sweat, while my breath hitches in my throat.

Millie saves me. She bounces up behind me with a bag of Doritos in one hand and a giant can of tea in the other. "Stop picking up hot guys at the gas station. I already told you that they don't like riding in the trunk." She glances up at Dean and holds his gaze as she says to me, "The shovel will smack him in the head every time you hit a bump."

I nod like she makes sense. Millie takes my arm and continues to talk, but that look in Dean's eye freaks me out. I'm barely breathing while we wait in line to pay for the goodies in Millie's hands. She leans in close to me and laughs, like I said something funny. She's nervous. Her voice is too strained. It's like she figured out what happened without me saying a word. "That's him, isn't it? The guy from last night? Your ex?" I nod and smile at her. At least I try to smile. My face feels like

I'm wearing a week-old mask that's turned to plastic. Millie laughs again and leans into me. "Let's pay for this and get the hell out of here."

The line moves slowly because no one is ever in a hurry. It drives me nuts. People materialized after we walked in and beat us to the counter. Millie continues to chatter as I glance around, looking for Sam. There's no sign of him. I glance around out of the corners of my eyes, looking for Dean. I feel his eyes on the back of my neck, but I can't see him—not without turning around. I don't want to do that.

It's finally our turn. Millie puts her things on the counter, and Mustache Dude rings us up. Millie pays, and we head out to the car. I glance over my shoulder and see Dean watching me as we walk out the door. He's got his hands in his pockets and is standing outside the store in a shadow. He waves at me.

"See you soon, Sid! I can't wait!" Dean calls out as I get into the car.

Millie finally acts like something is wrong. "Start the car. Let's get out of here. He's watching you."

I shove my keys in the ignition and twist. The car doesn't even try to start. My jaw is locked. Millie seems to realize it at the same time as I do. "He did something to the car."

I try to crank it again, but there's no power. My throat is too tight, and there are still goose bumps on my skin even though it's hotter than hell outside today. I feel safer inside the car. I don't want to get out, but I need to look under the hood. It feels like I'm in a trance. The world isn't spinning anymore. Time stops. I don't want to feel like this, and the only way to make it stop is to get away from Dean.

I kick open the door and get out. Millie does the same. I yank open the hood and look at my battery. One of the cables came loose. The cord is detached and lying there on top of the plastic battery case. I feel his breath on my neck at the same time as his voice. "Car problems, Sid?"

"Leave me alone," I growl at Dean before turning on my heel. I walk to the trunk and grab the tools I need to reconnect the cable. Who does stuff like this?

Dean's grinning ear to ear. "I can fix it for you and buy you pretty gals lunch, if you like."

"No. Go away." I plan on ignoring him, but Dean won't leave me alone. He keeps brushing into me, touching me like it's an accident. He follows me back to the hood and shoves in between me and Millie.

"We're fine," Millie tells him. "You should be on your way."

"Aw, how sweet. Your little friend thinks she can protect you. What happened to the teacher?"

"Fuck off, Dean." I'm mad now. I hate him. I hate everything about him, everything he's done to me. My life would have been so different if Dean never came along. I'd run him over with the car if it would reset everything, but it won't.

Dean feigns offense. "Who taught you to talk like that? Such a dirty mouth on such a pretty girl. Just the way I like it." He grins at me. Millie makes an annoyed sound. Dean ignores her. While I'm under the hood, Dean slips his hand over my back. His fingers tease at the edge of my shirt and brush against my skin. The touch makes me jump.

I don't think anymore, I just act. I swing my fist at his face and scream, "Leave me alone!"

Dean is smiling, acting like this is a game, until I land a punch on his cheek. Anger flashes in his eyes. He backhands me. The wrench goes flying out of my other hand. Millie screams, and I can hear the old clerk yelling, but there are no words.

Dean grabs my wrist and starts pulling me across the parking lot. "Walk or I'll make you wish you had."

I try to peel his fingers off, but I can't. I drop to the ground with the intention of making him drag me. My jeans save my skin from being torn up by the rocks and scattered debris. No one helps me, well, no one but Millie. She does something. Dean yells, and then he drops me. My wrist is burning where he was holding me, and my hand has cracked open.

I jump to my feet and look up in time to see him grab something from Millie and smash it on the ground. Millie tries to take it back, but he shoves her so hard that she falls. Millie is screaming. The old man is yelling. And Dean is standing in front of me looking really pissed off. "Get in the fucking truck. Now."

Someone yells that they called the cops. It's the woman with the bread. She's been inching closer and closer, but she's too old and small to do anything. "You better get out of here, kid."

Dean spits at her. The woman steps back. Dean hisses, "Go inside and let us finish this alone. This is a family matter." He sounds totally reasonable, but his actions don't match his words. The woman doesn't move.

My body is so tense that it feels like the muscles are going to snap. This is a new level of crazy, even for Dean.

"Sidney, I swear to God that I'll make you regret this. Your mother asked us to get you and you act like a goddamn bitch—" He reaches for me when a voice booms behind us.

"Get off of her." Every head turns. I half expect to see a police officer, but it's not. They aren't here yet. It's Peter, and he looks insanely pissed off. Millie's eyes widen, and her head twitches back and forth between Peter and Dean. Part of me is relieved that Peter showed up, but the other half doesn't know how to accept his help. Lucky for me that I don't have to decide.

Dean thinks that Peter is the timid professor from the other night. He doesn't realize the man standing in front of him is a Ferro. If Dean knew, he'd run the other way. The Ferro's are fierce, and Peter has been in more fights than his other brothers combined. There's no way to be that rich and not attract media attention when you punch your way from Manhattan to Fire Island. Peter's reckless behavior left behind a trail of people who would love to see the Ferros fall.

Dean steps in front of me. It's a possessive move. "Better go home and get your crush in check, Professor, or—"

Peter doesn't stop. He walks across the dusty parking lot, straight up to Dean, pulls his arm back, and swings. It's not a sucker shot, but Dean doesn't expect it. His neck twists to the side on impact.

Peter doesn't stop. He's not the same man he was last night. Something changed. Just as he takes another swing, Dean moves. The lunatic runs straight at Peter, and Dean rams his shoulder into Peter's stomach. There's an *oof* sound, and the two keep at it. Peter twists around quickly and manages to grab Dean by the throat. He pulls Dean close, so Peter's lips are nearly touching Dean's ear. Peter's eyes lock with mine as he says words that I can't hear. Dean's eyes narrow into slits as Peter chokes him, whispering threats—probably the same threats that made my brother turn pale.

The hot wind whips my hair away from my face. I brush it back, watching the two of them. I can't believe what I'm seeing. Peter's muscles are corded tight. His shirt is stuck to his body as beads of sweat roll down his temples. The look Peter gives me says so much, but this version of him scares me. Last night Peter didn't fight back. I want to know why. I thought that he wasn't a fighter, but not now. Peter Ferro can protect himself and anyone he cares about. Our gazes are locked. Only a second passes, but it feels like a lifetime.

That's when I hear the gun cock. I turn to look in the direction of the sound. The old guy with the crazy mustache is standing with a shotgun in his hands. He lifts it so that Dean and Peter are in his sights. The old guy spits on the ground, then wheezes, "Take this foolishness somewhere else. Now."

Peter looks pissed, but he releases Dean. The two of them step apart, but when their gazes meet it looks like they want to kill each other.

Dean backs away with his hands in the air. "I don't need this shit." He walks across the parking lot and slips into the truck. The engine starts, and he pulls away. I watch him leave, wondering where my brother was during all of this.

Peter and Millie are flanking me. They glance at each other before the old man drops his gun to his side and walks toward us. "Don't bring trouble around here again. You're not welcome. Get going."

Millie's mouth is hanging open. "We didn't—"

Peter shakes his head at her, trying to get her to shut up. He's polite to the guy with the gun. "I apologize." Then Peter glances at Millie and says, "Stop at the next rest area. I'll follow you."

I don't argue. I just grab Millie's arm and push her into the car. The old guy is watching me like the entire incident was my fault. Guilt climbs up my throat, because deep down it feels like he's right.

CHAPTER 5

Millie stares at me with her jaw hanging open so wide that I can see her tonsils. "Did you see that? Did you see Dr. Peter Granz—a friggin' English teacher—kick ass back there?" Millie tucks a curl behind her ear. She glances back at the black car following us and waves at Peter. He doesn't wave back. There's a scowl on his handsome face. "I heard he got his butt kicked last night. Did he? I mean, what the hell was that? He came in all vigilante style. I thought he was going to snap Dean in half."

"Peter didn't fight back last night. He's not—" I make an aggravated sound in the back of my throat. The rest area sign says it's a few miles away. I don't want to stop. I don't want to talk to Peter.

"He's not what? 'Cause, holy shit, that was so awesome I can't stop fanning myself. A guy rescued you!" She darts upright in her seat and corrects herself. "No, wait! He saved you twice. Sidney—"

"Millie, Peter isn't what he seems—"

She glances back. Appreciation is strewn across her face, like I landed the man that makes all other men look like monkeys. "I know…"

"You don't know! He's not. Damn it, Millie, pay attention." Millie turns around and looks at me, I mean really gives me a once-over. I'm so upset that I could rip the steering wheel off in my hands. "Peter is Peter Ferro. Do you know what that means?"

Her eyes slowly grow as big as dinner plates. She turns her head and looks back at the man following us. "Holy shit."

"You see it?" It's obvious once you know to look—the dark Ferro hair, the strong jaw, the stunning blue eyes, and that temper. All of the Ferro men have it, and the daytime talk shows love to point it out.

Millie nods. "He looks like the pictures I've seen. Everyone's seen him. Pete Ferro is hot. Why is he pretending to be a teacher?"

"I don't know what he's doing. Listen, no matter what he says at this rest stop, do not leave me alone with him. Do you understand? Nod and say yes."

She nods and gives me a crooked smile. "Fine, but—"

"No buts. Say yes. I don't care what he says or what he wants me to do. If Peter tries to get me alone with him, say no. Don't leave." Desperation floods my mind. Peter had offered to come with me. He wanted me to call the cops. He wanted to make sure I was safe, and this is how he finds me, in a parking lot in the middle of nowhere with Dean dragging me across the asphalt.

"Okay, okay. I won't leave, jeez." A wicked smile spreads across her face. "You know what they say about Pete Ferro; so is it true?"

I pull off the interstate and slow the car. There's a rest stop with picnic tables and a little brick building with restrooms. "Is what true?"

She giggles and leans in closer to me. Her hand keeps flying to her mouth, like she's embarrassed. "His dick—is it as big as they say?"

"Millie!" I stop in a parking spot and throw the car into park.

"It's not like you haven't heard it before. Pete Ferro, super lover to the supermodels, and their moms, and their friends, and their kitchen staff, and—"

"Yeah, I get it. He's a male slut."

"He's a strapping male slut who's done every woman from coast to coast." Millie's grinning like a love-struck teenager. She glances back at Peter.

"Shut up," I say and kick open the car door.

Millie jumps out after me. She places her hands on the roof. "Oooh! Testy! Are you protecting his virtue?"

I open my mouth, but Peter cuts me off.

"I have no virtue." Peter's window is down. He hears Millie as he pulls in the parking space next to us. He cuts the engine and gets out. Millie's face turns beet red. "She told you who I am?" Millie nods but doesn't look at him.

Peter walks around the car and comes straight at me. He stops short, like he just remembered what happened when I left. "Are you hurt?"

I shake my head. My heart is pounding. I lose all my bluster, which drives me nuts. In my head I'm roaring like a lion, but I sound like a mouse when I actually speak. "What are you doing here? Did you follow me?"

Peter smashes his lips together and then smiles at me, like he's really mad. "Yes, I did. I didn't think you'd leave without me. I didn't think you'd walk away in the middle of a fight."

"The fight was over. You said if I left not to come back, so I didn't."

Peter lets out a rush of air. His anger fades and he looks at me with so much remorse in his eyes that I want to melt into his arms. Peter considers me for a moment and then says to Millie, "You can't skip out on finals. Get back to the university before someone fails you."

"But there was an emergency and—"

"This doesn't count. You can't be nice to get out of finals. Every single professor will fail you." Peter tosses his car keys at her. Millie catches them. "Drive my car back. I'll stay with Sidney."

"No, you're not. Millie is coming with me, not you." I fold my arms over my chest. My head sways from side to side when I say the last two words. I may have lived in Texas for a few years, but I'm still a Jersey girl through and through.

Peter smirks at me, then says to Millie, "Toss me the bag on the front seat." Millie does it. I give her an evil stare. My eyeballs are bugging out of my head as I shrug with my palms up. It's a *what the fuck* pose and I mean every inch of it.

Millie beams at me. "I think this'll be good for you. You need to go, and it seems like you two have some issues to work out." I want to kill her, but I'm too shocked by her betrayal to speak. I just stand there with my mouth hanging open.

"And you," she says to Peter and walks up to him, poking him in the chest, "if you hurt her—if you lay a finger on her—I will get my daddy's gun and shoot you. It's a promise, not a threat." Millie is so small and pretty that it looks like he's being threatened by a china doll.

Peter grins at her. "Good. I wouldn't want it any other way."

"Damn straight." Millie looks over at me again. I'm so mad at her that I can't speak. My arms are folded tightly against my chest. She knows how betrayed I feel.

"Sometimes you need friends, Sidney. You can't do everything by yourself. Let someone help you, okay?" I don't say anything to her. Millie smiles awkwardly and slips into Peter's car, and drives away, leaving me behind.

Peter is standing next to me. He works his jaw before saying, "We need to talk."

"There's nothing to talk about."

CHAPTER 6

I'm sitting in the passenger seat, staring out the window at the night sky. I feel like an emotional train wreck. It's strange, but I thought I already grieved and mourned my mother. As I sit, memories that were lost to time pop up randomly in my mind. The hand of death is the only thing capable of freeing them. I see myself on a swing and know that I can't be more than three years old. My mother pushes me, and I try to look back at her, making my hair tangle in the chains. I can feel the sharp tug on my scalp like it's still happening. I remember the tears that covered my face and how afraid I was. My mother untangled me and held me. It's not a recollection that I would normally remember, but it surfaces now. My mother loved me then. I wonder what she'll say when I walk in the door now.

A chill races down my spine, making me shiver. It's late, well past dinner time. I rub the goose bumps away with my hands while trying to avoid Peter's gaze. We haven't spoken since the rest stop. I feel so betrayed by him. It's like someone turned me inside out. I hate that I feel his eyes on me. It makes me want to open up and spill my guts. I want my Peter back, but he's gone. That Peter was never real anyway.

After a few more exits pass, Peter pulls off the road. We're in a little town in Tennessee. It's so hilly here, the opposite of where we were in Texas where everything is as flat as a frying pan. I shift in my seat and look over at him. Peter has that same look he's had all day. I can't tell if he's angry or annoyed.

I don't care.

Yeah, keep telling yourself that.

Peter pulls into a dark parking lot and drives to the front of an old hotel located at the back. One yellow light floods the front door.

"What are we doing?" I don't want to stop here. The place looks like it's owned by Norman Bates.

"We need to stop for the night, and this is the only place showing any vacancy." He notices the expression on my face and adds, "Don't worry. It'll be fine. I've stayed here before." Peter cuts the engine and steps out of the car. Then he walks around, opens my door, and extends his hand, waiting for me to get out.

I really don't want to get out, but I do it anyway without taking his hand. Peter shakes his head slightly and then stretches as he turns away from me. His shirt lifts, and I can see his beautiful body, as well as the spot where it's marred by that horrible scar. The blemish makes me wonder. Peter can fight, but he didn't last night. I wonder if he fought back the night the knife was shoved in his side. It feels like there's more story there, something deeper that he didn't tell me.

Peter shoves his hands in the pockets of his jeans and looks back at me. Curiosity spreads across his face when he sees me gawking at him, but he doesn't comment on it. "Come on. Let's get a room and grab dinner. We haven't eaten all day and if I have to eat another cereal bar I'll—"

"You ate all the cereal bars four hours ago." It's the first thing I've said to him since we left. The teasing comment is light. For a second I regret it, but then I push past it. I have to decide what to do with him. I look at Peter from under the curtain of hair that's been hiding my face all day. Fuck it. The silent treatment isn't worth the effort. I reach into my pocket and twist my hair up into a ponytail. Stray curls are probably sticking out like Satan's horns, but I don't care.

Peter walks ahead and grabs the door. He holds it for me, and I step inside. The place seriously gives me the creeps. Peter walks past me to the front desk and rings the bell. An elderly woman, bent with age, hobbles out of the back room. She adjusts her glasses and smiles warmly at Peter like she knows him.

"Peter Ferro. I didn't think I'd see you in here again." Her wrinkled lips smile warmly at him before she glances back at me. "This fine man stayed here before. A Ferro chose to stay at my motel and not that other place down the road." She's beaming with pride as she tells me this.

Peter turns up the charm and cranks his smile to full wattage. He takes her hands and says, "Because this place is the best. I couldn't drive through here and not stop." I swear to God, the old lady blushes. Peter pats her hand before letting go. "How have you been?"

She smiles shyly and shoos at him. "You don't have time to listen to an old woman prattle. I bet you're famished. Here's your pass to get dinner in the restaurant. Each room comes with a hot meal. And here is the room key." The old woman turns slowly and takes a key off the board behind her. She explains as she's handing it to him. "It's the only room I have left. I'm sorry about that."

I don't follow, but Peter seems to. "It'll be perfect. Thank you so much." He hands her a credit card and she swipes it.

"Checkout time is nine, and since this room is the honeymoon suite, it comes with breakfast in bed. What time would you like that delivered?"

I nearly choke. "What? We can't stay in the honeymoon suite." I'm next to Peter at the counter now, ready to jump over the edge to look for an alternate option. "You must have another room."

"I'm sorry, dear, but we don't. There's a convention that has us all booked up. The room is very lovely."

"But it's a…" *Sex room! It's for happy couples, married couples. It's not for us!* I don't say any of it. The words bounce around in my head like bowling balls crushing every other thought. Instinct is telling me to keep space between Peter and me, but I can't, and this makes it worse.

Peter is grinning at me. "It's a…what, Sidney?" He's leaning on the counter wearing that tight T-shirt with a lazy, sexy smirk. I hate him.

"Nothing."

"No, you definitely thought it was something. Go ahead and tell us." He's teasing me.

My face heats up as a blush travels from cheek to cheek. Screw it. I say the first thing that comes into my head. "It's just that I'm sure it's a beautiful room and I don't want it to get messed up like last time. Peter has issues controlling himself. He makes love like a rabid monkey, and things tend to break. I don't want to ruin your best room. That's all."

Peter's mischievous grin widens, like the statement is true. I meant to embarrass him, but it obviously didn't work.

The old woman pats my hand, pulling my gaze away from Peter. She says, "I know, dear," and looks up at Peter and winks. The girlish look on her face implies that she intimately knows what I mean.

I blink twice, certain that I heard her wrong. It makes Peter laugh. He grabs the key from the woman and says, "Thank you, Betsy. I promise that I won't break anything while I make wild monkey love to my friend."

Peter pulls me through the door. When we step outside, the night air is thick and warm. It smells like honeysuckle and jasmine.

My mouth is hanging open. "Did you—"

Peter doesn't stop walking. He heads to the car and pulls out our bags. "Did I what, Colleli?"

"Did you sleep with her?"

"I've slept with a lot of people." Peter carries our bags to the room and slides the key into the hole. It's a real brass key with a big plastic tag hanging off the end.

"What the hell kind of answer is that?"

"It's the only answer you're getting, since you believe what you've read in the tabloids instead of what I've told you." Peter steps into the dark room, turns, and stops abruptly. I smack into his chest just as he drops the bags. His face is so close to mine that I can feel his breath when he speaks. "I fucked half the East Coast, remember? The women around these parts are very satisfied. I can add you to the list later if you like."

Anger surges through me. I hate the way he's talking to me. When he says the last part, my temper gets the better of me. My hand flies and my palm slaps him across his face. Peter doesn't even flinch. He catches my hand and presses his on top of it before I have time to pull away. He holds it there, and that lost look surfaces in his blue eyes.

Panic races through me. I still feel everything I felt for him yesterday and the day before. I still want to touch, kiss, and taste him. My heart beats faster as Peter leans in, closing the space between us. His lips linger so close to mine. If I move the slightest amount, we'll kiss. I don't breathe as my body tenses up. His hand, that slightest bit of touch, is shooting a current through my entire body. The way he looks at me makes my stomach flip. I hate the way he makes me feel, and I love it at the same time. I'm trapped, unable to move. The moment lasts forever. I think about closing the distance; I think about pressing my mouth to his and holding him again. My gaze is locked on his lips, and just as I lean in, Peter pulls away. He drops my hand and steps back.

"I'm not like my father—not anymore. A kiss means something to me, and I don't share them with women like you."

If he slapped me, it would have hurt less. "A woman like me?" He nods. "What the hell does that mean?"

Peter steps closer again, and lowers his face to mine. He speaks swiftly and passionately. "A woman who's blinded by my name, a woman who can't see me as anything but a Ferro."

I fight with him. I argue because I need it. I want to scream and slam my hands into his chest, so I do it. Peter doesn't move. His eyes are narrowed into slits like he hates me. "You fucking lied to me!"

"I'm still the man I was yesterday, and the same man as a week ago. "

"No, you're not! You hid the biggest part of your past and never told me a damn thing! You're a liar, just like him!" Just like Dean. He was all smiles and flattery until he turned on me. The scope of Dean's betrayal reaches out and chokes me, years later, and this feels like the same goddamn thing. I slam my hands into his chest again. This time Peter grabs my wrists and throws them aside.

He presses his forehead to mine and hisses, "I am nothing like him. How could you say that? After all the time we spent together, how could you—"

Tears are stinging my eyes, but they don't fall. "After all the time we spent together, how could you not tell me who you really are?"

Frustrated, Peter releases me and screams, "Because shit like this happens when people find out who I am!" He breathes hard and runs his hands through his hair, tugging hard. The saddest expression I've ever seen plays across his eyes when he sits down on a chair by the door and holds his head between his hands. "Damn it, Sidney, this wasn't about you. I just wanted to start over. It wasn't about you."

I watch him for a moment. I see the way he grasps his dark hair and then runs his hands over the back of his neck. I know he's hurting, and I hate that I'm the one who's causing it, but I can't leave things like this. "Tell me why you didn't fight last night. Dean deserved to be beat to a pulp, but you didn't. Why?"

Peter looks up at me. His eyes are the darkest shade of blue, nearly black. They pin me in place and strip me. I feel vulnerable and I hate it, but I don't move. The light from the open door spills into the room. It paints shadows across Peter's beautiful face, making him look harder than he is. "Why should I answer that? You're just going to use it against me."

I resist the urge to pull my hair and scream at him. Taking a deep breath, I manage to keep a steady tone. "There are two different versions of you that don't fit together. I'm wondering if I was with a lie for the past few months. I know you can fight. I know you used to fight all the time, but last night you didn't. It was intentional, and I want to know why."

Peter laughs so sadly that it breaks my heart. He stands up and steps over to me. Looking down into my face, he says, "I gave you the chance to know me like that and you threw it away. I don't give second chances, Colleli. You have no right to ask me anything like that anymore. Grab your wallet. We're going to dinner and you're buying whatever that voucher doesn't cover."

It feels like he reached into my chest and crushed my heart, but I don't show it. My face is utterly still, relaxed like I don't care. I nod and say, "Fair enough. You paid for gas all day."

The conversation ends, and we're miles away from where I wanted to be. In the back of my mind I'd hoped that it was possible to fix things with him, that Peter could convince me that he's the same person that he always was, but he doesn't even try. Instead, he shuts me out. I'm not the one who did this. My resolve to push him out of my heart solidifies. Peter Ferro will never know every part of me again.

CHAPTER 7

Dinner is slow and silent. By the time we head back to the room, I'm ready for a long hot shower. Peter unlocks the door and for the first time, he flips on the lights. I stop in my tracks just on the other side of the door. Peter rams into my back, nearly knocking me over. He grabs hold of my arm just above the elbow and steadies me.

"Holy shit." The room is…I have no words. My senses are overwhelmed with thick textures, red velvets and satins. There's a shag rug the color of a rose that covers the floor from wall to wall. One huge heart-shaped bed sits in the center of the room with a matching heart-shaped mirror on the ceiling. I'm standing there with my hands clapped over my mouth.

Peter shoves past me. "She's a nice old lady with interesting taste." Peter sits down hard on the bed and pulls his shoes off. He flicks his eyes up at me after a second. I haven't moved. "So it looks like a porn set from the seventies. What's the big deal?"

My eyes widen, and I look over at him. "There's a pole." I walk forward and slowly reach out my hand toward the brass pole in the middle of the room. I move carefully, like it might bite.

Peter has a crooked smirk on his face. "You're so prude."

I yank my arm back and turn on him. "Are you insane? This room would make a prude person have a coronary! They'd fall over on the bed and watch themselves die in the ceiling mirror. There's a pole!" My voice squeaks the last part.

Peter peels off his shirt and shakes his head. I watch him do it and wish I hadn't. His body is so beautiful that it's hard to look away, but I manage. My stomach does a little somersault just before I turn. "So hang your laundry on it and stop freaking out."

"What kind of married couple uses a pole on their wedding night?"

He grins. Peter pushes off the bed and walks over to me. He looks down into my face. He's standing too close, and from the look on his face, he's doing it on purpose. "I think you wouldn't be freaking out if you'd seen a pole dance before. You know the woman doesn't actually fuck the pole, right?"

My jaw drops. I make a high-pitched sound and slap his chest. "Yes, I know that. And I suppose you've seen plenty of dances on one of these."

"Yeah, but only at strip clubs." His eyes drink me in. They're so dark. He holds my gaze for a moment and adds, "How about a private performance?" I go to slap his face again, but Peter catches my wrist and stops me. It dawns on me that he could have stopped me last time, too, but he didn't. His eyes flick back and forth between mine. "Stop slapping me, Colleli."

"Stop giving me a reason to, Ferro."

Peter's look hardens. He drops my wrist like it's made of thorns, points to the bed, and uses a stern voice. "Sit." It doesn't sound optional. I wonder what the hell he's going to do. For once, I don't question him. I just follow his finger and sit on the edge of the heart.

Peter walks toward the pole and takes hold of it. He doesn't look at me. Instead his dark gaze is downcast and his long lashes hide his eyes. I don't know what I expect him to do, but he starts to move. I feel a smile spread across my face. "I know what a pole dance is, Ferro."

"Uh-huh" is the only thing he says. Peter moves around the pole, flashing his sculpted muscles at me. I roll my eyes and act like I'm bored. He smiles, but doesn't look up. It makes my heart pound. That shy smile is what drew me to him in the first place. It's one of the looks that Peter gives that makes me want to melt. At first I'm ready to laugh, but after that, something changes. The way he moves his body is titillating. I feel hot, and certain parts of me are demanding attention. I try to stop looking, but I can't.

When Peter reaches for the button on his jeans, I jump up and stop him. My hands fly to his before I realize what I'm doing, and how close I am to touching him in a way that I shouldn't. My pulse is pounding and everything sounds so much louder—my breaths, his breaths.

Peter freezes when my hands land on his toned stomach, right over his. Neither of us moves. For a second we just stand there. The compulsion to wrap my arms around him shoots through me. I want to feel Peter against me, but that door closed.

I shift and try to pull away, but Peter doesn't let me. I look up. Mistake. His eyes hold me in place, and all the air is stripped from my body. "No touching, Colleli."

"I wasn't…I mean, you can't strip for me." I remove my hands and step away, breathless.

He grins. "I wasn't.

"Then, what were you doing?"

"Taking off my jeans. I don't walk around commando. Do you?"

I shake my head. The thought terrifies me. "No."

Peter holds my gaze for way too long. The expression on his face says that he wishes things could be like they were. If he could rock-step his way back into my heart, he would. What he doesn't realize is that he's still there.

I shiver and turn away. I hate this room.

"You can wash up first. The bath is around the corner." He points at the red wall in front of me. I nod and grab my bag.

When I round the corner, I gape at a huge champagne-glass tub and keep walking. There's a door at the back. I assume the shower is in there, but when I pull open the door, it's only a toilet. Turning slowly, I look back at the monstrosity in the center of the room. "Peter…?"

"Yeah?"

"You want me to clean up in the sex tub?"

"You're in the sex room, Sidney. Get over it."

Fine. What an asshole. I poke around until I find the water and turn it on. I fill the huge glass tub, and look at the wall. From where Peter's sitting he won't be able to see me. I strip quickly and get into the glass tub. It's not as deep as it looks. My heart is racing. If Peter walks over, he's going to get an eyeful. There's nothing to conceal any of me. I wash as quickly as I can and nearly drown myself trying to scrub my hair.

After I towel off, I pull out my pj's. They're not guy friendly. I didn't expect to have anyone with me on this trip, and they were the pair I told Millie to pack. I have a threadbare white tank top and bottoms that are too short to wear. They're slightly longer than my panties, but they don't really cover anything. I don't want to be prude, so I tug them on and run a brush through my hair. I stand there way too long and look at myself. My headlights are on and very visible. I can't go out there and waltz by Peter like this.

"Come on, Colleli. I need to get in there." Peter's voice is coming from the corner. I know he's standing right there. I pull a towel off the rack and wrap it over my shoulders. It doesn't do anything to hide my butt, but it's the best I can do.

I try to walk past him quickly with my head down and my brush in my hand. Wet hair sticks to my cheek as I look at the floor. Peter's bare ankles catch my attention. My gaze flicks up and I see Peter standing there in his boxers. I want him to hold me so badly. I wish today never happened.

"Are you going to wear a towel to bed?"

"Yes and if you try to take it from me, I will kill you."

One of his eyebrows creeps up his forehead. "Feisty much?"

"No. Serious much. I didn't plan on having anyone with me. I packed comfy, which means this is old…"

"And filled with holes. Oh come on, Sidney. It's not like I'm going to judge you and your ratty pj's." He reaches for the towel, but I shriek and spin away.

"Don't touch me!" My heart is pounding violently. I clutch the towel tighter so he can't take it. I know I'm overreacting, but I can't stop. My emotions are short-circuiting and fear is pouring into me.

Peter steps back and raises his hands, palms up. "I'm not. I won't touch you. Sidney, I'm sorry. I didn't mean to…" His voice is so soft, so warm. I press my lips together hard and hold them like that. I'm afraid of what I'll say. Peter remains where he is. "I won't hurt you, Sidney. No matter what happens between us, I promise you that."

Glancing over my shoulder, I see his face and know he means it. My throat is too tight to speak, so I nod and walk over to the bed. I keep the towel around me and climb under the covers. I feel so stupid and afraid. I don't know if I'll ever be normal again, but I wish I were. I'm so sick of feeling this way, of overreacting. I can't read people anymore. I don't trust myself, and if I can't trust me, how can I trust them?

But Peter's in the same room with you.

But Peter's touched you.

But Peter…

It's always *but Peter.*

CHAPTER 8

My mind wanders in darkness, seeking out memories that I'm always trying to forget. Dean's face comes into focus. His vivid eyes glitter like emeralds. He holds my hand and whispers sweet words in my ear. I'm younger and unafraid. He says everything I want to hear. I smile and lean into him.

The grass turns to carpet under my feet, and we're in the mall. My heart beats harder; my mind knows this memory well. I feel sick, but I can't stop it. The dream continues, and Dean is holding my hand like he's done a million times before. He's walking toward his van at the back of the parking lot. I follow him. I trust him blindly. We get in the back, and he kisses me. Dean's lips cover my neck and trail down my chest. It makes me giddy and nervous at the same time. I'm not ready to be with him, not yet. I want him to slow down, but he urges me to go on, saying he loves me.

I hear his voice like it's next to my ear. "I love you, baby. I just want to show you."

"Dean, slow down." I'm still smiling, but I'm nervous. I love him. I want to be with him, I'm just not ready yet. The idea of giving myself to him like that scares me a little bit. I'll be connected to him for the rest of my life. The words echo in my head like a gong as Dean presses kisses to my throat.

"Let's play a game," he tells me and grabs a tie he has in the back of the van. Dean is lying on top of me. My shirt is gone, and so is his. His eyes keep drifting to my black lacy bra before returning to my face. "It's like the trust game we played when we were kids. I'd fall back and you'd catch me."

"Or drop you."

He smiles. "Exactly, but we're taking it to the next level. You fall first, then you can do it to me."

My stomach is swirling in knots, both good and bad. This scares the hell out of me, but I nod. Dean ties the blindfold around my eyes, and the world goes black. Then I feel something stiff wrap around my wrists. "Dean, what are you doing?"

"The same thing you'll get to do for me. Trust me, baby."

He ties my wrists together and tugs the seat belt all the way out. It snaps back, locking in place, holding me still. I'm blind to what he's doing, but it feels good. His fingers trace my curves, gently touching my stomach and trailing a line up to my neck. My pulse beats faster and faster. I like it. I like what he's doing and how he makes me feel. I'm not sure how much time passes but my wrists start to hurt.

He trails his lips to my waist and unbuttons my jeans. I stiffen and tell him to stop, but he doesn't. "It's your turn to fall, baby."

In that second, everything changes. Dean doesn't listen to me anymore. The more I tell him to stop, the faster he moves. He shucks my jeans, and they're gone, along with my panties. I beg him. The words flow from my lips over and over again. "Stop," but he doesn't.

He touches me anywhere and everywhere. He tells me that I can do this to him when he's done. I keep thinking that this isn't happening, that it can't possibly be real, but I feel his fingers push into me followed by a sharp pain between my legs. I try to lock my knees together, but he forces them apart. Dean's jeans are open and his hard length presses into me.

I retreat into my mind. It's the only way to escape. I stay there, half a world away, but it's not far enough. Dean says things but his voice is muffled, lost in ecstasy. *It hurts, it hurts, it hurts.* Tears stream from my cheeks and I stop yelling. I whimper, silently waiting for it to end. But I don't know that it'll ever end, that this will replay over and over again every time I close my eyes. Dean shudders and goes still. He rests on top of me, breathing hard as I cry.

The dream blurs, fading to black, but my heart continues to race like it's going to explode. There are arms around me and a soft voice in my ear. Peter holds me, saying soothing words that don't register. I'm not fully awake, but I'm not asleep. I'm caught in between. My towel is wrapped around me, but I feel Peter's warm skin on my arms. He holds on to me with his face nuzzled in my neck. My cheeks are cold and damp like I've been crying forever. I wish it would stop, but it never does.

Drowsiness overtakes me and pulls me back under. Dreams swirl around me, but they don't ensnare me this time. The night passes, and when I wake up, I'm in the bed alone. I stretch and sit up, looking for Peter. He's lying on his back at the foot of the bed with a pillow under his head, breathing slowly, still asleep. I watch him for a moment, wondering if he was really next to me or if I dreamed it. If I was braver, I'd get up and lie down next to him, but things can't be like that anymore—not for us.

CHAPTER 9

Peter is driving my car and I'm staring at the side of his face, lost in thought. He ignores me for a few miles and finally says, "Can I help you with something?"

I blink a few times and try to look the other way, but the sun is still low on the horizon and totally blinding. "No, I was just trying to burn a hole in the side of your face with my laser vision. It didn't work."

He smirks. "Very mature"

I raise my hand to my eye, line up Peter's face in the center, and pinch my thumb and forefinger together. "No, this is mature. I'm squishing your head. Go on, say something else and I'll do it again, bitch. I'm not afraid to use these puppies." I pinch a few more times while giving him the evil eye.

Peter slows the car and pulls over to the side of the road, brakes, and throws it in park. "Get out."

"What?" Is he insane? We're in the middle of nowhere just after sunrise on an alien abduction road.

"You heard me, Colleli. Get out. Now." Peter kicks open his door and slams it shut. I wonder what the hell he's doing, but I don't follow.

"It's my car, asshole! You can't tell me what to do!" Peter is at my door. I startle, and my heart tries to leap out of my chest. He yanks the door open and I practically fall out.

"Yes, I can." We're standing on the side of the road in the tall grass. Bugs are buzzing along with something else that I can't identify.

I get to my feet and glare at him. "What are you doing? You can't just stop the car and get out."

He looks at me like I'm crazy. "I kind of did..." A truck blasts past us, swallowing up the rest of his words and throwing my hair in my face. Peter's lips continue to move, and the next thing I hear is, "last night, so you're driving for a while." He shoves past me and sits down hard in the passenger seat.

What an asshole! He snaps at me to get back in the car. I grit my teeth together and hurry around to the driver's side. I leave my windows down and let the wind blast me for a while. When I can't stand it anymore, I blurt out, "Why'd you come?"

Peter has his arm over his face and is slumped back in the seat. He peeks out from under his elbow. "Excuse me?"

"You heard me. Don't pretend that you didn't. Why'd you bother showing up if you're just going to sit there and be pissed off for two thousand miles?" He doesn't answer. Instead, Peter covers his face again and acts like he's going to sleep.

"Hey!" I smack his shoulder. "I'm talking to you."

"Why do you think? And stop hitting me. You're going to catch me off guard and I'll accidentally punch you in the face or something. Now, stop talking and let me get some sleep, all right?"

My pulse picks up the pace. Maybe I wasn't dreaming. "You didn't sleep well last night?"

"No." He doesn't move.

I throw around the idea of asking him if he was next to me, but I'm fairly certain he was. I'm the reason he didn't sleep last night. "Thank you," I say without looking at him. I stare blankly at the road.

This makes him look over at me. "For what?"

I press my lips together. I don't want to say it. I don't want to thank him for anything, but I should. Especially that. "For last night. I know you woke me up and calmed me down. Then you acted like it never even happened. I kind of suck at that. So thank you."

Peter puts his arms down. He's quiet for a long time. Scruff lines his cheeks, and his hair is a mess. He looks more like the pictures of Pete Ferro from the paper now. "Sidney, I…" His voice trails off as he sits up in his seat. "You better change lanes."

There's a flock of birds on the highway. They're sitting there sunning themselves like they're movie stars. I wave him off. "They'll move."

Peter is staring at the birds as he speaks. "I acted like it never happened because I didn't want you to think I was trying to take advantage of you." His hands lift to the dashboard and he wiggles in his seat. "You might want to slow down and go onto the shoulder."

"Are you afraid that I'll hit a bird? Do you know how hard it is to hit a bird, never mind a whole flock?"

"Yeah, well, I'm pretty sure you could do it."

"What does that mean?" I straighten in my seat and glance over at him.

"Do I really need to explain that after the squirrel attack? Seriously, Sidney, move over. One of those things looks like a turkey." Peter tenses and keeps looking between me and the road.

"There are no turkeys sunning themselves on the highway." Just as I say it, the flock of birds takes off, just like I thought, except for one huge bird that decides to walk across the lane.

"Uh, Sidney—"

"Why isn't he flying?" The bird is as big as a shopping cart and seems totally happy to be sitting in my lane. What the hell? I'm almost on him by the time I realize that he isn't going to fly away. I brake hard and swerve the car, but the damn bird keeps walking. It screeches like a cat in a trash compactor as the car nearly mows it down. I miss the bird and swerve onto the shoulder as we skid to a stop. Heart pounding, I turn around and look back at the damn bird. Peter gives me a look that says *I told you so*. I point a finger at him and say, "Not a word."

He grins. "I didn't say a thing."

"Who expects to see a goddamn turkey in the middle of the highway?"

"Uh, me. I told you, 'Hey Sidney, there's a turkey in the middle of the highway.'"

I glance back at the thing, and the animal is still in the lane like he's perfectly safe. If it was later in the day, he'd be splattered by now. "What the hell is wrong with him?"

"He must be one of those suicidal turkeys I'm always reading about."

Ignoring Peter, I kick open my door and walk back to where the demented bird is still happily gobbling in the left lane. "Here turkey, turkey. Get off the road, you retard." I make noises like I'm calling a cat.

Peter walks up behind me. "What are you doing?"

I stand up straight and the turkey looks at me, but the fat bird doesn't move. "Damn, he's stupid. I can't leave him there. Get something from the car to get him off the road."

"Like what? You didn't pack any food and I doubt he wants a Red Bull."

"I don't know. Go find something."

Peter walks back and digs around in the trunk. He comes back with something in his hand. I can't really see what it is by the way he's holding it. Peter stops in front of me. "You want me to save the turkey, right?"

"I can do it."

He holds up a hand and walks onto the highway. I keep glancing down the road, waiting for signs of life. Peter moves toward the bird slowly, and when he's a step away, he throws something pink at it. My face scrunches together when I realize what he has—my bra. A strap lands over the bird's head. Peter yanks and the bird comes toward him. Peter scoops the beast up and holds him under his arm while wrapping the other end of the bra around the bird. It holds his beak closed for the most part so the thing can't peck at us.

When Peter hands me the turkey, it looks like the animal is wearing a pink padded push-up bra. "Here's your bird. Nice bra, by the way."

I'm frowning. The bra looks better on the turkey. As we talk a few cars pass by. "What's the matter with him?" I look at the thing, but I can't tell. He doesn't flinch when I touch him, like his wings are hurt. "Are turkeys supposed to fly?"

"I don't think so, but I'm not sure. I'm not into livestock."

"Well, it's good to know you haven't screwed everything on two legs." Peter mutters something, but I ignore him. "He doesn't look like a turkey, except for his gobbler thingie here." I point at the red lump hanging from his beak.

"Gobbler thingie?" I give Peter a look and head back to the car with the bird in my arms. "Where are you bringing that?"

"To a vet. He should have flown away."

"Sidney." Peter grabs my elbow and turns me around. "You can't bring that with us."

"Why not?"

"It's a wild bird. If he takes that bra off, he'll peck out our eyeballs."

"You couldn't get my bra off, so I don't think he will. I'll buckle him into the backseat. It'll be fine."

Peter follows after me. "I did get your bra off, mostly."

"Mostly doesn't count," I say as I lean into the car and put the bird on my back seat. For a wild animal, he really doesn't seem to mind the car, or being held. Maybe he's somebody's pet. "Do you think he's a turkey? I mean, he's really dark." His feathers are so brown they're almost black.

Peter sighs. "I'm an English teacher, Sidney. It's not a raven or an albatross. After that, I'd be guessing."

I laugh lightly. "Ah, famous birds in literature."

"Something like that." Peter glances at the bird. "We're seriously going to drive to Jersey with a bird wearing a bra in the backseat?"

"Yeah, I know someone there who will patch him up for free."

Peter slips into his seat and pinches the bridge of his nose with his fingers. "Wonderful. Now's a great time to become a philanthropist."

I slam his door and lean in through the open window. Peter glances over at me. "Who says that I wasn't before? I almost had pity sex with you. Talk about scraping a carcass off the road." I wink at him and walk around the car.

When I get in, Peter is watching me. "How flattering."

"I'm all about the flattery."

"And I'm all about the chivalry. I saved a turkey for you, you crazy person."

I glance in the rearview mirror. My turkey is looking out the window and wearing my best bra. I start laughing and can't stop. Every time I look back there, the image hits me hard like I've never seen it before. I have a turkey doing boudoir poses in my backseat.

CHAPTER 10

Peter won't recline his chair. Instead he sits there in the passenger seat with his eyes mostly closed. I can tell they're still open because his lashes flutter every now and then when he blinks. It's well into the second day and the sun is setting. I'm so tired, and I know Peter is exhausted since he won't sleep with the turkey behind his head.

"It won't bite you."

Peter keeps his eyes sort of closed with his arms over his chest when he answers. "That's very comforting, but I'd rather not risk it."

"I'm starting to think you have a bird phobia." The corner of Peter's mouth twitches like he wants to laugh, but he swallows it back down. The turkey shifts in the backseat and settles down again. Peter's eyes open until the animal stops moving. "Did Big Bird give you nightmares or something?"

"Or something," he says and closes his eyes when the bird stills.

What the hell does that mean? I glance over at Peter. The dashboard casts a soft glow on him and showcases the definition in his beautifully sculpted arms and face. The pit of my stomach fills with regret, and I have no idea how to get rid of it. I decide to press him a little bit, but I doubt that he'll answer. "So what made you decide to be an English teacher?"

Peter lifts his head and glances at me out of the corner of his eye like it's a stupid question. "I like to read."

"Wow, what a wonderfully profound and elaborate answer. Thank you for shedding light on that decision. I think I'll be a teacher when I graduate so I can be like you. You changed my life." I'm teasing him, and right up until that last point my words feel light and playful, but those last four words are real. I don't realize it until they tumble out of my mouth and fill the air like lumps of lead.

Peter watches me lazily from under dark lashes and shakes his head. "Nice, Sidney, real nice."

"We've been sitting next to each other for two days and you've hardly said anything."

"Neither have you. The only time you talked to me like this was when we were getting your passenger back there." Peter jabs his thumb behind us.

Awkwardness creeps up my spine. It feels like there's a hand on my jaw, forcing it open and making me speak. "I don't know how to talk to you anymore."

Peter straightens a little. "You realize what you've done, right?" I glance at him quickly and wonder where he's going with this. "Unbelievable. You don't know, do you?"

"Then educate me, teacher-man. Tell me what I did that was so hideously wrong." My hands grip the wheel tighter. This is why we haven't spoken in two days. It's because every time I open my mouth, we fight, and I'm sick of fighting.

"You turned on me. As soon as I told you my name, you acted like one of *them*." Peter stares straight ahead and works his jaw. I know he wants to say more, but he doesn't.

I keep my eyes on the dark road, watching the dotted white lines zoom by. "I did not. You didn't lie to them, whoever them is."

Peter cringes. "Nice grammar."

"Fuck you, Ferro. You lied to me, like majorly lied to me. You pretended to be somebody else from day one and never clued me in until you had to."

"That's not true."

"Psh, right. If my brother didn't show up with Dean, you wouldn't have told me at all. I would have found out and felt just as stupid and used later when some reporter figured out who you are. After everything that happened between us—" I press my lips shut and lock my jaw. *Stop talking.* I know I'm going to say things that I shouldn't say, things that I'll regret.

Peter sighs and tips his head back against the seat. "I would have told you, Sidney. I wanted to tell you, but it's not easy to talk about. You out of all people should realize that."

"Yeah, I do. I get it, but the thing is, I told you what happened to me. I told you all of it. You only told me half. If you don't trust me—"

"That's not it."

"Then what is it? Oh my God, say something! You just sit there brooding all day like a disgruntled supermodel. What the hell is wrong with you? Just say whatever it is you have to say!" I'm so mad at him. I haven't spilled my guts to anyone the way I did with him, and Peter held back. I can't stand it. I can't tolerate the notion that he knew me inside out and I don't even know his goddamn name.

"I can't, Sidney! I just can't!" He's yelling now, his hands flying like they don't know where to go. "I screwed up, I know that. Nothing I say will fix it. Nothing I do will show you how sorry I am. I lost you, but you're sitting right next to me!" He grips the dashboard and turns to look at me. "You've destroyed me. I thought I could handle this, I thought I could—"

Peter's rant gets cut off. He glances behind us at the same time flashing lights do the disco in my rearview mirror. Peter glances at me and slides down into his seat with his hand over his face. "Shit. How fast were you going?"

I cut him an evil look as I pull over. I have no idea. I want to scream and punch. There are a million emotions that are fighting to break free inside of me. I lock my jaw as I stop the car and pull over on the grass at the side of the road. I put down the window and sit there with my hands on the top of the steering wheel where the cop can see them.

He takes his time walking over. It's a state trooper. He's an older guy, skinny with weathered skin and angular features. He leans in and looks into the car. "License and registration please…" The man blinks like his eyes are broken and then tips the end of his pen at the backseat. "What are you two doing with that animal?"

Oh my God. I forgot about the bird. "Taking it to the vet. He's hurt."

The man looks at me like I'm crazy. Then his gaze shifts to Peter. "Sir, what are you doing with that bird?"

"What she said. It can't fly and was wandering back and forth on the interstate. My friend didn't want it to become roadkill."

The officer gives me a strange look as I hand him my cards. He looks at them and says, "Not many people would save a bird like that, Ms. Colleli."

"I know. They would have asked for a fork and eaten it."

The trooper's face scrunches together and he leans forward. He looks at the bird again. "No one eats those things. They're living garbage bins for roadkill."

"What do you mean? It's a turkey."

The man straightens and laughs, like big loud belly laugh. Peter glances at the bird and then back at me. He shrugs. The trooper is still smiling when he bends over again. "That's a vulture, a turkey vulture."

He tries not to smile, but I can tell he wants to. "Can you tell me why he's wearing a bra, miss?"

"My friend is afraid of birds and I didn't have anything else to tie him up with."

The man's eyebrows lift up to his hat. He addresses Peter. "Is that true, sir?"

"Yes." Peter gives me a look. The officer's eyes narrow as he looks at Peter. "What's your name, son?"

Peter leans back into his seat like he doesn't care. "Dr. Peter Granz."

The man continues to stare like he's trying to place Peter's face. "And you didn't know what type of animal this was, a man with your level of education?"

"I can't really dissuade this woman from doing something once her mind is set on it."

The officer glances at me and then back at Peter. "Well, I know what you mean." He's quiet again and then he flinches like someone splashed water on his face. Recognition grows with his smile. "You highly resemble someone—you're Pete Ferro, aren't you?" Peter smiles and nods. "Well, why didn't you tell me that?" The state trooper continues to talk, and I sit there and listen. Peter is clearly uncomfortable with the attention, but he smiles all the same. He talks with the man, the same way he would with anyone else. It's clear that the cop is a little starstruck.

When the cop finally is ready to leave us, I'm handed a warning and told to slow down. "Make sure she does it, Mr. Ferro."

Peter smiles and waves. "I will."

I put the car in gear and pull out, accelerating slowly. Peter slouches back down into the seat and presses his thumbs to his temples. I look at him out of the corner of my eye and say, "So I totally forgot about the turkey."

Peter glances up at me. There are dark circles under his eyes. His expression is worn, beaten, and totally stressed out—but when he looks up at me he smirks, then the smirk turns to a smile, and he laughs. "You rescued a vulture."

Peter starts laughing and I can't stay silent. Giggles erupt inside of me. I'm too tired and too stressed and this seems so funny.

"And you put him in a pink bra." I can barely get the words out. Tears blur my vision and my stomach hurts by the time I stop laughing. "God, he had to think we were nuts."

"He thought you were nuts, Colleli, not me."

"Do people always act like that around you?"

"What? Fake?" I nod. It was like the officer morphed into a shiny version of himself. His words were excited and filled with flattery. It was like an instant wall and there was no way it could come down once it shot up. "Yeah, most of the time. I did the scruffy look when I was younger. That's how most people remember me. If I stay cleaned up, I might look like a Ferro, but they don't usually ask me outright like that."

I nod, thinking. Glancing over at him, I say, "You don't trust anyone either, do you?" Peter is back in his defensive I-don't-care pose with his arms across his chest. It's a shut down, fuck-off stance.

"Not so much, no."

The laughter is gone. It's been sucked from the car and in its place is this empty, hopeless feeling. Keeping my eyes on the road, I start to ponder out loud. "We're so messed up, Peter, and it's not fair. But life's not fair, is it? There are no do-overs no matter how much you wish for them."

Peter watches me in the darkness. I can feel his eyes on the side of my face even though I don't turn to look at him. "Keep going forward, Sidney. Looking at the past only drags you back into it."

"Yeah, but you can't learn from it if you don't look back."

"You've learned everything you need to know."

I smirk at him. "No, I haven't. How could you think that? I made a mistake with Dean and I did the same damn thing with you. I can't judge character, like at all. I was totally wrong about both of you."

My words hit Peter hard. I might as well have swung a crowbar into his stomach. He doesn't look at me. "That's what you think, that we're the same?"

"It's the same deception at the heart of it, isn't it?" I'm seriously asking, because the hard part of my mind says yes, but there's a spot with a softer voice that says Peter is not the same at all.

"Maybe. A lie is a lie." Peter stiffens and shuts down.

I wish I hadn't said it. "Maybe. Maybe not. Why'd you do it?"

Peter's gaze cuts to me. It's so sharp, so bitter, that I want to look away. "I didn't want you to know. You're right, okay? We both lied to you, we both took things we shouldn't have, and neither of us is sorry for it."

I blink slowly like he didn't just say that. I can't breathe. It's like his words were a fist that shot straight into my stomach. There's an exit right in front of me. I nearly pass it, and decide to get off at the last second. Peter doesn't say anything when I change lanes abruptly.

We stop in front of a motel and I pull up under the overhang. Fuck this. I wish I left Peter in Texas. I kick open my door and go inside and get us a room. Peter doesn't follow.

When I come back out with the room key, I see him shake his head and end a phone call. He runs his fingers through his dark hair and looks back at Mr. Turkey. I slip into the car and look back at the bird. "You untied him, sort of." The bird is still wearing the bra, but his beak is free.

"Yeah, he wanted to talk."

I stare at Peter for a moment, wondering what could possibly be going through his head, why he's here, and what he wants from me. "Why did you insist on coming with me?"

Peter looks at me like he's tired of the question. "I already told you."

"Saying *you already know* isn't a reason. Tell me. Just say it."

Peter shakes his head and smiles. "Fine. You want to do everything on your own, but you can't. When you're around that guy, Dean, it's like your brain shuts down. You get sucked into your past before you can blink. I read your poem, I see it on your face, and I know what'll happen if he gets you alone. He's not getting you alone." Peter's gaze locks onto mine as his words burn with intensity. I need to swallow, but I can't.

"You're all about the chivalry." I used to tease him about that, but now I'm not.

"Something like that."

My heart is in my throat. We stare at each other for too long and our gazes melt together. Neither of us can look away. It's like we're both lost, drifting aimlessly, getting torched by life and everything that's happened to us. When my pulse is slamming in my ears like twin drums, I look away. It feels like there's a rubber band on my head and it pulls me back, but I refuse to turn.

I park the car. When Peter turns and gets out, I follow him into the motel room. There's a small double bed, no shag rug, no kinky sexy tub. It's just a plain old motel room.

CHAPTER 11

Peter's phone rings and he disappears outside while I take a shower. When I come out, I clutch the towel around my shoulders to hide my sheer pajama top. My hair is still dripping with that just-crawled-out-of-the-gutter, tangled look. I need to wait for Peter to jump in the shower so I can brush the tangles out.

Peter's gaze flicks up when he walks inside. He sees me standing there looking like a drowned rat. "I untied the vulture and put him down in the grass by the car.

Since he's crippled, I don't think he'll go anywhere."

"But what if a cat gets him?"

Peter lifts a brow at me. "I think the cat needs to be the worried one in that scenario. He'll be okay. He survived up until now on his own." Peter clears his throat as he walks over to the bed and digs through his bag. He pulls out a pair of sweatpants and looks over his shoulder at me. "My brother called back. Would you mind if we took a detour through New York? I need to get something from him."

"What part of New York? What do you need to get?" I sit down on a wicker chair by the door.

"The city, so it's not too far out of the way, but it'll probably add a day to our trip." Peter shucks his shirt as he's speaking and tosses it in his bag. When I don't say anything he looks over at me. My eyes are locked on his abs. Each one is clearly defined like Peter does a thousand sit-ups every day. "My eyes are up here, Sidney."

I startle and blink as my face burns from the rapidly spreading blush. The corners of Peter's mouth tug up. I hate that smile. It makes me want to do stupid things. Peter walks over to me with that confident swagger and stops. His boots are nearly touching my toes. He bends at the waist and lowers his face to mine. The movement makes me nervous. I try to sit still in my chair like I don't care what he does, but I can't even lie to myself—I'm attracted to Peter on a carnal level. It never shuts off, and it's annoying as hell. I swallow hard, wondering if he's going to kiss me. His lips are a breath from mine, and he's still wearing that sexy smirk.

"Yes?" I manage to say. Thank God my voice came out. I feel like I'm made of raspy panting sounds and that's it.

Peter's gaze dips to my lips, where it lingers way too long. The tension between us makes me want to giggle or punch something. Energy is building throughout my body as my stomach twists into curls. I want to lean in and kiss him. I want his arms around me. I want to run my fingers over the dips and curves of his chest, but I don't. I just sit there and raise a brow at him, waiting for him to do or say something.

"Hmm? Oh, nothing. I just thought it'd be easier for you to not treat me like man candy if my eyes were closer." Peter flashes a wicked grin at me.

My lips contort into an O and then a playful smile. "Jackass."

Peter doesn't move. He stays right there, and when he speaks his lips nearly brush mine. "Ogler."

"Pushy."

"Leerer."

"Jerk."

"Gawker."

"Jackass."

He grins. "Nice comeback, and you already used that one."

"Shut up."

"Make me." Peter looks so perfect, so utterly kissable. "Make me, Sidney." His voice drops to a whisper that's barely a breath when he says it. His sapphire eyes drift to my lips before returning to my face. He stays there, watching me from under those dark lashes.

My lips tingle, wanting his touch as my heart races faster and faster. Suddenly, I have no words and can't remember how to talk. Heat creeps across my body like someone pulled a blanket over me after taking it out of the oven. My fingers twitch as I think about slipping them through his hair. Oh God, why is he doing this to me? It's torture to have him so close and not touch him.

Two can play this game. I lift my hand to his cheek, and he freezes. As soon as my palm touches Peter's skin, that overly confident expression fades from his eyes. I trail my hand over his cheek slowly. Neither of us breathes as the pads of my fingers travel over the scruff on his cheek and down to his jaw. I lean in, like I'm going to kiss him. At the last second I push his face aside with the hand that's on his jaw and step past him with a satisfied smile on my face.

I think that's it. In the teasing contest, I'm the clear victor, but Peter catches my wrist. He gently stops me. That confident smile slips off my face as I turn back to him. Peter takes hold of my face with one hand on each cheek and dips his head. My entire body tingles, waiting for that kiss. Our eyes are locked together, each of us daring the other. Peter lets out a jagged breath and inhales again slowly. I feel the warm air on my face.

Last time we were like this, the idea of being with him scared me, but now I'm curious to see if I could do it, if I'd like it. My body is humming, but no one moves. It's like there's a glass wall between us and neither of us can break it. Peter's lips linger just in front of mine, parted ever so slightly. As his lashes lower, his gaze is singularly focused on my mouth. My eyelids feel heavy when he gently touches me. Peter's hands slip back into my hair and down my neck to my shoulders. He lifts one hand and caresses my cheek again.

I'm trembling all over by the time he does that. I don't know what I want. For some reason, I still trust him—but I don't. It feels like there are two women living inside my head. One is touch-starved and the other is too independent to want anyone, for any reason. She's fighting me, wildly throwing every image, every misguided memory at me, but I can't move. I don't want to pull away, so I linger, enjoying his touch and the feel of his breath across my skin.

Peter blinks slowly. Every time his lashes close, I think he's going to kiss me, but he doesn't. My heart pounds harder in my chest, making me feel crazier by the moment. His hand strokes my cheek again, and I clutch the towel hanging over my shoulders harder.

This time when Peter's lashes lower, he closes the distance. His lips brush against mine so lightly that it feels like a breeze. I tense as he does it, but Peter doesn't deepen the kiss. Instead he pulls back and looks into my eyes. The expression on his face makes me press my knees together to stop the current that's pulsing through my body. He makes me want things I never wanted.

It feels like I'm coming undone, but I don't feel scared, not this time. I do something crazy and lean in. I brush my bottom lip to his and shudder as I do it. Peter's hands are on my neck again, playing with the edge of the towel. He watches me for a moment and leans forward slowly. When his lips touch the side of my face, I inhale deeply and close my eyes.

Peter's kiss is so light, so soft that it makes me want more. I blink slowly like I'm half asleep. It feels like I'm floating, and I don't mind so much. It's scary, but the fear isn't choking me the way it usually does. I don't think about anything. I push the thoughts away, because nothing is the same anymore. The way Peter touches me is nothing like Dean...*He's nothing like Dean.*

The thought frees me. I rise up on my tippy-toes and take his cheek in one hand as I press our lips together. My kiss isn't light, like his. It's breathless and demanding. Peter's palms cup my face as the kiss deepens. I lose myself for a blissful moment. There are no thoughts, no worries. There's just Peter and his warm, soft lips that are kissing me so perfectly that my knees feel weak.

When he pulls back Peter is all jagged breaths. His forehead presses to mine as he watches me from under his lashes. I'm breathing too hard as well, but the more I try to control it, the worse it gets.

Peter's eyes drop to the place where I'm holding the towel around my shoulders. He watches me as he lowers his hand and takes hold of mine. I think he's going to take it away and I tense, but he doesn't. Instead Peter holds it tight and tells me, "Let go. I'll hold it for you."

His words hit me so hard that my jaw starts to tremble. Tears prick my eyes as I try not to cry. I've wanted to reach up and hold his cheek in my hand and run my fingers through his hair, but I can't do any of that if I'm holding on to the towel.

Peter realizes what his words do to me. He leans in and kisses my cheek gently. The kiss gives me courage. I'm so nervous that he'll put the towel down, that he'll let it go, but the offer is too much to ignore.

I'd wanted to touch his face, but when I release the towel and he holds it in place for me, my hands drift down to his chest. I drag my fingers over the toned muscles, feeling him beneath my fingers. Before I drift my hands down his stomach, I rub my thumb over his nipple, feeling the tight little bit of skin under my hand.

Peter inhales deeply, but he doesn't move. He blinks slowly and continues to watch me as my hands drift farther south. I feel each taut muscle of his stomach until I'm stopped by the waistband of his jeans. I trail my thumbs along his stomach and around to his back. I feel the scar on his side as the pad of my finger moves over it. I wonder if he feels the memory when I touch that spot. Scars never heal, and every time one gets touched, the memory that made it flares to life. I'm like that, but this is so different than anything I did with Dean that there are no memories to recall, no scars of tender touches to try and repress. This is new for me.

Peter's eyes close as my hand moves over his waist. I know the memory is flashing behind his eyes because he becomes rigid in my arms. I want to make it better; I want him to forgive himself for what happened. When he opens his eyes again, they lock with mine and his sorrow is no longer hidden. It's reflected in his eyes with so much regret that it's difficult to maintain his gaze. I'm no longer blinking or breathing.

The vulnerability on his face makes me do it. I lift my hand to the spot where he's holding the towel. I take his hand in mine and pull it away. My heart beats harder, but I don't let go of him. Peter doesn't look when the towel slips from my shoulders and falls behind me. I can't hide the tremors that shoot through me. I feel naked in front of him, even though I'm not. Peter's wearing less clothing than I am, but I feel so exposed. If he hadn't reacted that way when I touched his scar, I couldn't have done it.

But I did, and now I'm standing there in a threadbare shirt with my nipples at full attention. I don't want him to look, but I want him to. As I breathe in, my chest brushes against his. The contact without the towel in the way shoots through me like a bolt of lightning. My breath catches in my throat, and when I look up at him, Peter seems equally speechless.

His head dips again and he kisses me harder this time. His hands are on my face and then in my hair. They drift over my shoulders and down my back, gliding over the fabric as his tongue does wicked things in my mouth. The pit of my stomach falls down an elevator shaft and hasn't hit the bottom yet. I can't breathe like a normal person. I sound like I ran a marathon even though I haven't taken a step.

Peter breaks the kiss. Between breaths he presses his lips to the sides of my face softly, gently. His hands remain on top of my shirt. He doesn't lift the hem and slide his hands under. Instead, he presses his body against mine as he kisses me senseless.

I hold on to him tight, digging my nails into his back so he doesn't fade away. Peter nudges my face to the side as he trails hot kisses down my throat. My head falls back and I close my eyes, feeling each kiss as his lips press into me over and over again. When he stops, I look up at him.

Peter's lips are parted, and he's breathing hard. "We should stop."

I nod. "We should." It's something I know in my mind, but my body doesn't want to acknowledge it.

Peter makes the decision for us and steps away. He runs his hands through his hair like it's torture to stop touching me. When he looks over his shoulder at me, his eyes fixate on my chest.

I stand there, ramrod straight, and let him look. I know he can see the outline of my excited breasts and the pale skin tones through the shirt. Nerves swirl in my stomach, but I don't move. Peter doesn't look away. His eyes stay glued on my chest.

After a moment, I manage, "My eyes are up here, Professor."

Peter's gaze lifts slowly and meets mine as a sinful smile spreads across his face. "Say that again."

The corner of my mouth tugs up as I lazily point toward my face. "My eyes are up here."

Peter steps toward me but doesn't touch me this time. He stops within arm's reach. A dimple surfaces on his cheek, and I have the insane desire to lick it. My eyes flutter away from the spot and lock with his. "No, the other part. Call me *professor* again." Peter looks hopeful, more like the man I met in Texas. The look he's giving me is like the one he had when we were dancing.

I can't help but smile girlishly. I look up from under my lashes and whisper, "Dance with me, Professor."

Peter's smile broadens. He holds out one hand and I take it, while the other hand slips around my waist. If he was anyone else, I'd worry about his boots crushing my toes, but Peter never steps on me. We rock-step a few times before he spins me away. When he spins me back, I twirl into his chest, where he holds me tight. My hands slip around his waist and over the scar. I watch as Peter's eyes fill with memories he can't control. The smile fades like a star in sunlight, until it's completely gone.

Peter blinks a few times, like he's waking from a dream. He releases me and turns away. When he grabs his sweats off the bed, he bends over and picks up my towel. Peter turns back to me and places it over my shoulders and holds it tight in front until I take it.

He gives me a sad smile and says, "Thank you."

I nod slowly, not understanding. It feels like rejection, but in the back of my mind I know it's more than that. He's stuck, trapped in his past as badly as I am, or possibly more.

"I know there's no future for us," he says. "I screwed things up too badly in the past and I get that, but I really need a good friend right now and I know you do, too. This"—he inhales deeply and gestures between us—"can't happen again. I know that, but—"

I cut him off. I walk over to him and kiss his cheek before saying, "Peter, shhhhh. I'm your friend at the very least. At the very most, why don't we just wait and see?"

He looks at me like I'm a mirage. His eyes are so wide, so vulnerable. "I'm not the man I was before. I'm not Pete Ferro anymore." His eyes dip to the scar that wraps around his side. "You don't understand—she changed me in a way I'd never thought possible. I stopped fighting, I stopped doing all the shit that I was known for. Finding the right person is the kind of thing that you only get one shot at, and I fucked it up. I lost her.

"My life changed that night and no matter what I do, I can't get things back the way they were. Then I met you, and I thought I was wrong." He looks up at me, looking completely lost. "When I saw Dean, something snapped. If the old guy hadn't pulled out his gun, Sidney, I don't know what I would have done. I can't tell if I was justified or not, but every time I see that guy it's like…" He squeezes his hands tightly and swallows whatever he was going to say.

I watch him because I can't look away. This feels like a moment where everything is bending to the point that it's going to snap. I know what he means; I know it too well. I'm afraid to touch him, afraid to step forward, but I manage. My hand slips onto his forearm. The muscles are corded tight as if they'll break at any moment. Peter twitches when my skin touches his. He gazes down at my hand and then up into my face. "You're not Pete Ferro anymore. I get it. I'm not the same Sidney that walked around Jersey all those years ago, either. What was taken from us, we don't get back, Peter. It's just gone. It's like the land after a fire, charred to pitch black and barren."

He shakes his head. "No, not for you. Somehow you pulled out of that for the most part. I see it in your eyes."

"I'm wearing a towel to bed, Peter." I give him a sad smile. "I know I'm mental. I accepted it. I trust you and I still can't drop this thing." I tug the towel tighter around my shoulders.

"You did before."

"That was different." I look away. Emotions run through me with an intensity that makes me want to run into the woods and live with my turkey. I step away from him, but Peter takes my hand. The connection doesn't break. As long as he's touching me, it feels like he can see inside my head, and that scares me more than anything. There are monsters in there, memories I don't want to remember.

"Why?" His voice is so soft and kind. It's like cashmere, delicate and enticing. If I answer him, that voice promises too many things that I thought I'd never have. My lower lip quivers involuntarily. Peter's gaze fixates on the tiny twitch and he lifts his hand and presses a finger to my lips. His eyes flick between his finger and my eyes.

"Tell me." His finger slides away, leaving my mouth open and gasping like there's no air.

"I…" I can't say it.

I want to tell him, but I can't. I close my eyes and look down, but Peter doesn't let me stay that way. His hand slips under my chin, and he tilts my head back. Our eyes meet and the rest of the world melts away.

I want to be brave for once. I want to say it and see what happens. I've treated him so badly and he was so mad at me. Fear keeps shoving the words down my throat, but they rise up again, rebelling like they have a mind of their own. I feel the sentence on my tongue and then on my lips. "It was different before—I could drop the towel—because I was thinking about something, something I shouldn't." My lips part as I stand there trying to find the right words. "I got lost in the moment."

Someone sucked all the air out of the room, because I can't breathe. I feel like a fish on a hook with Peter's hand holding my chin up. He doesn't free me; he doesn't take the words and throw me back. Instead he leans in kissably close, and breathes, "Oh? What were you thinking that would make this feel safe enough to trust me like that?"

There's a knot in my throat that I can't swallow down. He has me reeling, dangling from the end of the pretty pink string, and it's all I can do to not back away. This conversation terrifies me, but it excites me, too. His hand is warm, gentle but firm. It moves from my chin to my cheek. I lean into his touch and close my eyes. "For a moment everything felt right, like things never happened. You seemed to latch on to the girl I was and pull her back. She's not afraid of you, and she's still in here wanting things I don't normally want."

"Tell me what you wanted, Sidney." Peter's eyes search mine, looking, hoping beyond hope.

My jaw hangs open, but no noise comes out. It sounded so different in my head. Saying it out loud solidifies the thought and makes it real. Peter brushes his lips over my cheek and pulls back. His eyes drift to my lips like he's thinking about kissing me again. I want to be brave, so I say it and tell him, "I wanted you."

A shy smile drifts across his lips. "Like wanted me, wanted me?"

A blush paints my face red. I feel the burn creep across my cheeks and can't contain my smile. I try to look away, but he won't let me. Peter's finger is under my chin again, tilting my head back so our gazes meet. "Maybe."

"When you say maybe, it usually means yes."

I grin. "Maybe."

CHAPTER 12

The rest of the night passes slowly. I toss and turn on the mattress, but I can't get my body to settle down. Having Peter at the foot of the bed makes me crazy. I want his arms around me, but I'm afraid I'll go nutso and tell him to get lost if he touches me wrong. I roll onto my back and pull the pillow over my face. The towel is a lump under my back, all bunched up and horribly uncomfortable. I'm smothering myself with the pillow when I feel it being pulled away.

Peter looks down at me with those gorgeous eyes. "Restless night?"

"Maybe." We both laugh softly. *Damn it. I had no idea I was doing that.* I make a mental note to stop saying maybe when I'm thinking yes.

Peter offers his hand. I take it, and he pulls me from the bed. I try to reach back for the towel, but Peter closes his eyes. "Leave it. I won't look." He holds his arms out, open. "Dance with me."

I tuck a piece of hair behind my ear. "Peter, I—"

"You said maybe. Maybe means yes. But you'll have to lead since I can't open my eyes." Watching Peter, I make my decision. He's bare chested and wearing a pair of gray sweatpants. I can barely see him in the darkness. The streetlight casts a yellow glow through the slit in the curtains. It illuminates his toned body and open arms.

I step into the space and take his hands. I put one on my waist and slip my palm in the other. Our fingers lace together and we start a slow rockstep. My heart is pounding even though we've done this a million times. In the past Peter was my teacher and my boss. Now he's half naked with his eyes closed. *How'd we get here?* I never would have thought this is where we'd end up when I first met him that night at the restaurant.

Just as I calm down, something scrapes the door. It sounds like a nail slowly dragging across the metal. Peter's eyes burst open as I cling to him. I forget about the towel and my ratty pajamas. That sound is just wrong, like a switchblade dragging across metal—or like Dean's knife. I glance up at him just as Peter looks down at me. Neither of us says anything, and then the sound comes again.

Peter releases me, leaving me at the foot of the bed. He presses his finger to his lips and waits for me to nod before moving away to look out the slit in the curtains. Peter stands there for a moment, careful not to touch the fabric. He pads back to me and whispers, "I don't see anything. Maybe they've gone." But just as he says it, the horrible sound comes again. It's louder and longer this time.

My mind is messing with me, throwing me into the past. Glints of silver flash behind my eyes. I press myself to Peter. "That knife, Dean's knife…"

Peter holds me tight. I can tell he doesn't want to let go, but the sound comes again. Maybe he's carving something into the door. Maybe he'll finish and go away. Peter whispers soothing words in my ears but never takes his eyes off the door. I chant *go away* over and over again in my mind as if it could actually do something.

Peter's hands firmly hold me against his chest. We watch the door, waiting for it to fly open, but silence fills our ears. Swallowing hard, I look up at him, ready to speak when something bangs into the door and at the same time the knob rattles like someone is trying to open it. Frantically, I look around the room for something to defend us with, but I don't have anything. My pulse is roaring in my ears, so when Peter lets go of me and strides toward the door, I freak out.

Peter is livid with testosterone flowing off of him in crushing waves. The scar on his side flashes pure white as he crosses the strip of light on the floor. It flashes over his body like a grocery store scanner. Before I can say anything, Peter hurls the door open. It smacks into the wall so hard that the knob smashes a gaping hole.

Peter steps outside. "Come out, you motherfucker, and settle this now!" His fists tense at his sides as he walks farther into the parking lot, barefoot. The lights in the room next to us flip on. I see the golden glow on the ground outside their window, spilling into the parking lot.

I want Peter to come back. I can't lose him. I can't. I race after him when something darts out from behind a bush next to the door. It rams straight into me, running over my bare feet with claws.

I scream and fall back, trying to get away from it before I realize what's happening. Peter rushes toward me and stops. A huge smile breaks across his face, and the worry evaporates. I'm still scooting back like I'm being attacked when I finally stop and look at the thing sitting on my legs. My turkey vulture looks back like I'm crazy before walking over me. It scrapes its beak on the metal door, making a hideous noise, and then slips into the room.

Heart pounding, I look back at Peter, "What the fuck?"

Peter has his arms folded across his broad chest. "Well, it appears that the big bird of prey doesn't want to sleep in the parking lot."

I'm staring, still not believing it. *Why?* "Why does this shit happen to me?" I jab my thumb at the people watching us in the next room. "It doesn't happen to them."

Peter nods and waves at them with a smile he tries to cover with his hand. The people disappear back into their room. "Well, for starters, they didn't take a lame bird off the highway and let it wear a bra all day. If you ran it over like a normal person, we wouldn't be having this conversation." Peter is so close to laughing that he can't keep a straight face. "By the way, next time I'm saving you from a giant chicken, stay inside."

Peter drapes his arm over my shoulder and walks me back inside, closing the door behind us. "You were going to fight whatever was out there, weren't you?" He nods. "What makes a man turn pacifist and then back again?"

"A knife in the side changes a guy." Peter looks around for the turkey. It's under the sink, preening. "Uh, Sidney. I'm not sleeping on the floor with that thing in the room. I'm not even sure if I can sleep with that thing in the room."

"Then throw him outside."

Peter looks back at the animal and then at me. He laughs and shakes his head. "No thanks. Besides, he'll just do it again."

"A cat probably tried to eat him."

Peter lets out a loud laugh. "He probably ate the cat and the dog that was chasing it. Now, he's ready for bed. If you look really close at his beak," Peter is pointing so I lean forward to see what he sees, "you can see the white tip of a cat's tail."

I slap his shoulder and laugh. "You're an idiot."

"You're going to invite me to bed."

My face goes blank. "Excuse me?"

"I'm not spooning with a vulture. God knows what he'd do with my little bits."

A smile creeps across my face. "They're little? That's not the kind of thing a girl likes to hear."

Peter sits down next to me. "You realize the reply to that comment is that you should come and see for yourself, right? Do you really want me to say that?"

I try not to smile. I try to look serious but the corners of my mouth twitch. "Maybe."

Peter laughs and reaches for me. His fingers tickle my sides lightly and I fall back onto the bed with Peter leaning over me. "Can I sleep with you, Miss Colleli?"

"That's rather forward, Dr. Granz."

"I'll keep my hands to myself. I promise."

"You'll keep everything to yourself." He looks at me, confused. I explain, "When I was younger and I first heard about sex I thought it sounded disgusting. I couldn't imagine why anyone would ever do something like that, ever. But babies are really cute and come from somewhere, so it must happen on its own."

"On its own?" Peter gives me a confused look.

"Yeah, like *it*"—I gesture toward his package—"sneaks over in the middle of the night while they're both sleeping and does the deed on its own."

Peter lets out a loud laugh and hugs me hard. "I'll keep it in my pants, Colleli."

CHAPTER 13

In the morning as Peter loads up the car, I flip open the room bill. I blink at it a few times as the bird waltzes out of the closet or wherever he slept and jumps into the car. I think he adopted me, but I'm not really sure.

I fold the top of the page back and look at Peter. "There's a $250 charge on here for something. Did you order a bunch of porn after I fell asleep?"

"No, and for that price I could get a hooker. Let me see that." Peter slams the trunk closed and holds out his hand.

Placing the paper in his grip. "Yeah, a hooker with a peg-leg, maybe."

He doesn't look over at me. "You'd be the one to get a pirate hooker, not me. The eye patch turns you on."

My jaw drops open and I gape at him. "How could you say that?"

"Because it's true. Admit it, you like the idea of a guy wearing a pirate shirt with burly forearms with the smell of the sea on his skin." I don't say anything. Peter looks up at me and drops the paper to his side.

"You just described half the guys in Jersey. Damn, Peter, I have better taste than that."

"Really?" I nod. He glances at the car and then taps the bill with his fingers. "You sure about that? I mean, you have a pet vulture."

"He's a turkey. He's just misunderstood, that's all."

"He's going to eat your face off in the middle of the night, and the $250 bucks is a cleaning fee because this hotel is supposed to be pet-free."

I pout without thinking about it. "He's not a pet. He's an accident victim. Something ruined his wings."

"I'll take care of this and then we can go." Peter starts to walk off toward the front of the motel. He stops when I call after him.

"You're right, maybe. I would like you in a pirate shirt."

Peter turns around with a wry grin on his lips. "Oooh, talk dirty to me, baby."

"Maybe."

Peter presses his hand to his heart and pretends to lose his footing. "Not here in the parking lot. How can I control myself when you have a mouth like that?"

"It's the lips you have to watch out for." I blink after I've said it, not realizing how dirty that sounded.

"Sidney, please! You're going to make me blush." Peter winks at me and jogs the rest of the way to the front.

I climb in the car and look back at the bird. "You're going to be a pain in the ass, aren't you?" The bird has his head turned backward with his beak under a wing. It looks wrong. Heads are supposed to face forward. "You need a name. Let's see…"

Peter returns to the car quickly and slips into the driver's seat. It's really cute with the way he bounces into his chair and beams at me. Dark hair falls forward into his eyes, making them seem bluer than gemstones. I forget what I'm thinking and get lost in the moment.

Peter grins at me. "Ogler."

I smile hard and look away. "You like it."

"I didn't say that I don't. In fact, you can fondle me with your eyes whenever you want."

I snort laugh and settle back into the seat after pulling up my feet and putting them on the dashboard. "Wow, what a pick-up line."

"I don't need a pick-up line. I've already got you, and if memory serves me correctly, you're the one who came onto me." Peter pulls the car out of the parking lot and heads for the interstate.

"Mmm, so you've said. So back in the day, was it a normal thing for you to take home random girls that sat down at your table?"

An embarrassed look flitters across his face and disappears in a blink. "Maybe."

"So the newspapers saying you were a playboy, those reports were…?" I'm fishing, trying to get a feel for his past. I want to know more about him. I pick at a spot on my jeans with my finger and look over at him from the corner of my eye.

"An understatement. I uh…" He lets out a rush of air and glances at me. "What specifically are you asking?" Peter seems nervous and grips the steering wheel harder.

"Rumor has it that you punched or screwed everyone you came across for a while."

"I punched guys and screwed women, not the other way around. Tell me that's not what you're asking—I'm not bi and I don't hit ladies." He glances at me quickly and then returns his gaze to the road.

"Good to know." I become silent, trying to figure out what I think of him and how it fits in to what I already know.

"What about you?"

"What about me?"

"Same questions—do you have any bisexual inclinations or punch random women? I could get on board with both of those, ya know."

The corners of my mouth lift. "You're so stupid."

"You didn't answer, Miss Colleli."

I shrug. "Up until I met you I thought I was broken. The idea of being with anyone like that wasn't appealing."

"And now?"

"Now, I might be tossing the idea around a little bit, maybe." I grit my teeth together and mentally scold myself as my face grows hot. I bend over and press my face into my knees.

"I told you that you like coming onto me. I think we should play it this way." I glance up at him, loving that he didn't comment on my red face. "I won't have sex with you. You're the one who decides that stuff, and I'll follow your lead, okay?" He takes my hand and squeezes it. "Thinking about it isn't bad, you know. It means you're moving on."

My mood deflates like a balloon. I glance out the window after taking my hand back. "No, I'm not. I'm just tired of waiting to get over it."

"Sidney, you're farther down the road than me. I'm going to lose sight of you soon. I think you're right: we don't really forget what happened, but we accept it and learn to live with it. I haven't done that yet, at all, but you have and you are. I wish…" His voice trails off. When I glance at him, I notice how tight his jaw is, like he locked it to keep from speaking.

"Tell me," I say gently and reach for his hand. His palm is hot, but the skin on the back is cold to the touch. I thread his fingers through mine, wishing I could erase his pain.

He smiles sadly. "Sometimes it feels like I'm standing at the brim of a mental cliff. My toes are over the edge, and the slightest wind will knock me off balance. I know I'll fall, but I can't back away. That's my life. That's my brother's life, except he went over the rim. I don't want to end up like that. If I stand there, I know I'll fall, but I can't seem to back away." He inhales slowly and lets out a shaky breath without looking at me.

Trees zoom past the windows as the turkey rustles in the back seat. The animal makes a noise and goes back to sleep. "Yeah, I know what you mean. For the first couple of years, it felt like I fell into a gorge. My stomach was in my throat all the time. I was worried about what would happen to me when I hit the bottom."

"You think you hit the bottom?" I nod. "What was there?"

I think about it for a second and smile at him. "You were there. That night in the restaurant, that was the bottom of my pit. That ended the free fall, and everything shifted." Peter nods, but doesn't say anything. "You can't control everything; take it from someone who knows. Let go a little bit and see where you end up. It might not be so bad."

Peter squeezes my hand and lifts it to his lips. "I don't deserve you."

"I didn't think happiness was in the cards for me, but then I met you. You deserve a reprieve from anything you've done that's chewing you up inside. Stop thinking so much and see where life takes you. Who knows, you might end up in a car with a crazy girl and a cross-dressing vulture." Peter smiles warmly. I scoot into the middle seat and lean my head against his shoulder.

CHAPTER 14

When we hit Pennsylvania Peter stops for gas. I run into the ladies' room while he fills up, and on the way out, I run into my twin—like literally run into him. Sam steps in front of me and I smack into his lean body. I look up, ready to apologize, but then see who it is.

"So you came." Sam's hair is hidden under a ball cap. He's wearing an old track T-shirt from high school with a pair of jeans. It's the same look he had before I left home. Sam's shoulders slump forward slightly from fatigue. He glances toward the refrigerator case at the back of the store where Dean is standing with his back toward me.

I keep moving toward the door. I'm not having another altercation at a mini-mart. "Of course I came." I make it to the front of the store and push outside. The door trips a bell that makes my blood run cold. I feel Dean's eyes on me. They drift over my back like a cold claw, but I don't stop. *Get in the car. Get in the car. Get in the car.*

"The guy's with you?" Sam looks around for Peter and sees him standing by my car, refueling it.

"Obviously. I'll see you at home."

Sam nods. His gaze narrows when he looks at Peter. "I don't like him, Sid. He seems a little off, like he might snap and go postal or something."

"Then don't piss him off." I finish speaking as I reach the car. Peter looks up, and anger flashes in his eyes when he sees Sam. "Come on, let's get out of here." I slip into my seat quickly and pull the seat belt across my lap. I don't need to say anything to Peter. He takes my cue and leaves, but not before staring both men down. I wonder if Peter is unstable, but brush away the thought. We're all unstable to some extent. Having someone watching my back isn't a bad thing.

After we're on the road, Peter asks, "Did he touch you?"

"No, not really. I walked into Sam. Dean didn't say anything. He just watched me like a creeper." Chills run over my skin. I smooth them out with my hand, but it takes a while for them to go away. I glance back at the turkey and wonder if he's dead. "He doesn't move much, does he?"

Peter glances up into the mirror. "Only at night when I'm about to have sex with you. It's like we have a chaperone." Peter seems tense, like he has liquid anxiety flowing through his veins instead of blood. "We're going to have dinner with my brother tonight, if that's all right. I need his help with something."

I nod, not really understanding why he's nervous. I keep looking behind us, wondering how far away Dean and Sam are. "Which brother is this?"

"Sean, the eldest. My younger brother is a free spirit, but Sean is more down-to-earth. He's dealt with shit, which is why I want to talk to him." Peter looks fine, but his voice is a little too tight, and his hands are at ten and two on the steering wheel. He only does that when he's pissed or worried.

"What do you want to talk to him about?"

"You and me. I don't want to share your pain with anyone, and maybe I won't have to, but Sean is kind of unpredictable. I need to know if I can mention what happened with you and your family—and Dean."

"You trust him, even after he killed his wife?"

"Yeah, but I have to say that I don't know what happened that night. No one does. Sean never spoke about it, but I don't think he killed her. He was so excited about the baby. It just doesn't make any sense." He's quiet for a moment, thinking.

I wonder what would drive someone to kill. I hate Dean, but I don't want to kill him, not when I'm rational or awake anyway. But if Dean got hit by a truck, I wouldn't lose any sleep over it. I wonder if that's the same thing and suppose on some level it is.

I glance at Peter. "Say whatever you want. I just don't want the whole story plastered all over the Internet in the morning. And I don't want to hear it when you tell him, either. Tell me to go to the bar or something." My stomach flip-flops inside of me. I hate the idea, but if Peter feels like he needs his brother, I think it'll be good for him.

Being cut off from my family freed me in some ways, but I regret it. I didn't want things to end that way, but I had no idea how to fix it. This is a chance for Peter to mend fences with his brother. I want to encourage it even though the name Sean Ferro sends ice down my spine.

―――――

We get to New York pretty late. Peter calls his brother when we get to the hotel. We shower and dress quickly. As I'm applying eyeliner, I see Peter walk by behind me. He has a towel around his waist and his hair is damp and tousled. From where I stand, he can't see me unless he looks up in the mirror. The wall outside the bathroom extends into the room, giving the illusion of privacy. I freeze and wonder if he saw me change before. I can't remember where he was standing, but I don't think it was over here.

My eyes dart toward movement and I catch sight of Peter dropping the towel. He stands with his back to me, totally naked. The eye pencil hovers as I blink rapidly, taking him in. Peter's body is perfection, except for that scar at his waist. The gash is a thin white line that extends down and wraps around his side. His back is all muscle, but I knew that before.

What I'm staring at—what I can't rip my eyes off of—is that perfect ass. He's all toned muscle, every bit of him, and that butt is no exception. My mouth gapes open as I stare, wondering what it would be like to have that naked body sliding against mine with my nails biting into that perfect behind. There isn't a rational thought in my head. I just stare, thinking about feeling every inch of him beneath me, wondering what that would be like. That's when he bends over to grab his boxers and I nearly die. A breath catches in my throat as I shift my position in front of the mirror to get a better view. That's when I manage to jab the pencil into my eye.

Peter spins around to see what happened, thinking that I can't see his gorgeous naked body. I squeeze my eye shut and mutter expletives. When I look up I can see his beautiful blue eyes in the glass, they lock with mine, and a wicked smile spreads across his face. "Were you watching me, Miss Colleli?"

"No, I just thought about that pirate thing you said last night, so I—" *What the hell am I saying?*

"So you stabbed yourself in the eye?" He's walking toward me, which makes me so nervous I can't stand up. My heart hammers inside of me as nervous energy races up and down my arms. I slam the pencil onto the counter and blink repeatedly, trying not to look at him. I've never had any interest in looking at a naked man before. I never saw what all the fuss was over. I mean it's not like that whole hairy package area was appealing, but oh my God—on Peter it's completely…Ideas ricochet off of my mind and simultaneously bounce in a million directions. I want to touch and slide my hand along his stomach, my lips tingle as I think about kissing him below the belt, and my tongue—it's like I've lost my mind. Totally foreign thoughts whirl through me and rip away things I put on my *I'll never do that* list.

Before I realize he's crossed the room, Peter is behind me. He steps close to my back and looks over my shoulder at us in the mirror. One of my eyes pretty much has a black line over it since I drew on my face after I stabbed myself. I look ridiculous, but I so don't care. His naked proximity shoots tension through every bit of me.

"You were watching me, Colleli."

"You're nice to watch, Granz." I say it too confidently, as if I look at naked men all the time. Then, I point to my red eye and say, "I hope you have a thing for pirates. I'm pretty sure I—" An involuntary noise emerges from my throat as Peter puts his hands on my waist. I'm so high strung, so lust ridden, that I can't think. We watch each other in the mirror.

Peter's eyes are so dark. His voice is deeper than usual when he speaks. "Turn around, Sidney."

I shake my head even though I want to turn and look. I'm so lying to myself. I want more. I feel it coursing through me. I don't want to look; I want to touch and do things that I never thought I'd do. Oral sex doesn't sound so bad at the moment, and I wonder about it for a second. Before now, I wasn't interested in anything, and the idea of sitting on some guy's face or kneeling and sucking his…I can't even finish the thought. My lips twitch as I consider it, which makes the sexy smile on Peter's face brighter.

Peter hesitates, but then slowly lowers his lips to my neck. His mouth brushes against me lightly when his hands slip to my shoulders. The touch is gentle but firm. My head tips to the side, and I close my eyes. Peter pulls away but doesn't release my shoulders. I glance at him in the mirror. The only thing I can see is his chest. "We better get dressed and go downstairs." I try to nod, but my head doesn't actually move. My God, he broke me. I couldn't form a coherent sentence right now if I wanted to.

I try, and my tongue tangles in my mouth. "They'll think we're not coming."

Peter's lips twitch. "For someone who's never made love, you use a lot of double entendres." He winks at me before kissing my cheek and crossing the room. A shiver tickles the skin on my back, running down my spine and landing between my legs with a tingling that won't stop.

What he said doesn't register at first, and then when it does I shrug and smile. "Wait to see how many I throw around after we're together."

"Is that a promise?"

There are no maybes this time. I look at him in the mirror and nod. "Yes."

CHAPTER 15

Peter takes my hands as we emerge from the elevator. Nerves flitter through my stomach. This hotel is way posher than any place I've ever stayed. It's daunting and makes me feel like my black dress is substandard. Peter is wearing a suit that he had with him. The only reason I have the black dress is that I anticipated needing it for my mother's funeral; otherwise we wouldn't be able to get into the restaurant here. I didn't pack any cocktail dresses. Peter's brother picked this hotel because he's been staying here.

Peter explains, "Sean is in town for business, but he stayed longer than usual. He hates New York. The guy shows up once a year and leaves as soon as he can." He glances at his watch. I'm starting to think that Peter is intentionally stalling, which is fine by me.

As we exit the elevator, I can see the swank restaurant in front of us. I hesitate. My feet slow, and Peter stops and looks over at me. I hate to state the obvious, but someone has to say it. "We can't afford this, Peter. The hotel cost a small fortune for the room. How are we supposed to pay for dinner too?"

"I'm a Ferro, Sidney. We have deep pockets."

"But you walked away—that money isn't yours anymore. The estate is your little brother's."

He pats my hand, "I have enough to last a while, so don't worry about it."

I tease, "What, do you have a trust fund somewhere that I don't know about?" He nods like it's nothing. "You're rich without being the heir?"

"I was trying to separate myself from the Ferro name and make it on my own."

"And I screwed that up." I lower my eyes to the floor as guilt chokes me. I ruined his life.

Peter lifts my chin and looks me in the eye. "You are exactly what I was looking for. It wasn't isolation or even walking away from my family—it was you. I needed you. I'd burn the trust fund and walk away right now if that's what it takes to show you how much you mean to me." Peter looks toward the hostess, who's been smiling at us from across the room, and then back at the elevator. "Come on, let's go. Forget this. I don't need Sean for this." Peter starts walking away.

I can't fathom what's going through his mind, but he tried to get this meeting with Sean multiple times. Walking away now would be silly. I don't even know what Peter hopes to gain by this meeting. I doubt it's going to be a hug-fest. I don't move. He stops and looks at me. "Money doesn't matter to you, does it?"

"I can always earn more. There are other things that are more precious. I guard those with my life."

The way he looks at me says everything. He means me—that he wants to protect me and take care of me. This meeting with his brother has something to do with protecting me, at least that's the way it seems. "Sidney, I have enough to get us through this. Come on, let's get out of here."

I shake my head and look back at the hostess. "No, this is what you wanted to do. I already made a mess of your life. I don't want to do it again."

Peter smiles at me. "You don't realize how much you're worth, how wonderfully perfect you are. You saved me, Sidney. I can't repay that debt, ever. You didn't screw up my life. You took a broken man and revived him. No one else could do that. It was you, it's always been you, since the first time I saw you walk into that little restaurant in Texas and you circled the floor. You have no idea how lucky I felt that you sat down at my table. You're an amazing woman."

I suck at receiving compliments, and that is the longest, most awesome compliment I've ever gotten. I want to look away, but Peter leans in and kisses me instead. It makes it easier to accept his words. I feel like all I do is take from him, and that I don't give him anything back, but maybe that's not accurate. I let the thought rest. I'll deal with it later. "I love you."

He kisses my forehead and says, "I love you, too. You ready?" I nod and we walk off to meet the craziest Ferro of them all—Sean.

CHAPTER 16

Peter walks past the hostess, and says we're meeting someone. She offers to walk us back, but Peter is already cutting across the incredible room. I'm not sure where he's going until Peter slows as he comes to a table. Peter cuts through the restaurant from the side and approaches a man with his back to us. Peter must have circled the perimeter until he caught sight of his brother. I can't see Sean, and I'm nervous. I can't imagine what this must be like for Peter, but he seems unfazed.

There's a woman seated across from Sean. I can see her perfectly. She's leaning forward, with her dark hair spilling over her shoulders, saying something to Sean when she glances up. She stops speaking and stares at Peter as we approach. Peter is in front of me as we step up to their table.

The grip on my hand tightens a little bit and then releases. I stay a step back as Peter greets his brother. I wonder what they were like as children, if they knew how tragic their lives were going to be. No child thinks that anything like that will happen. The future is always bright; it isn't until you get there that you realize it isn't.

Sean introduces his brother to the woman at the table. "This is Pete Ferro."

Peter corrects, "Actually, I dropped the Ferro part. It's Dr. Peter Granz."

Sean's voice is deeper and more jaded sounding. "You took her name?"

Peter nods. "It felt right after everything that happened." Peter changed his name to hers after she died. That's so tragic and beautiful that I have to fight the *awwwhhh* that wants to crawl up my throat. I wonder what it does to him. Hearing her name every day must remind Peter of the life that slipped between his fingers.

They say a few more things before Peter looks over at me and pulls me forward. I've been hanging back like a wallflower. The woman across from Sean has been watching me, but she doesn't say anything to me. She's polite and asks if the men are twins. She looks like a model. Her hair has no frizz and her makeup looks like it was painted on by da Vinci. "This is Sidney Colleli."

Sean stands and turns to look at me. At that moment I see the striking similarities between the Ferro men. They look like photocopies, but Sean's eyes are different, harder. He inclines his head to me. "Good evening, Miss Colleli."

"Please, call me Sidney."

"Very well, Sidney." Peter pulls out the chair next to Sean and my heart flip-flops. Even if Peter doesn't think Sean is nuts, I'm not ready to breathe easy around him. I lower myself in the chair and then Sean sits back down. Peter takes the seat across from me and smiles. It's a look that says *don't worry*.

Sean glimpses over at me and says, "This is Avery Stanz, my…" I wonder why he hesitates. I look at the woman and an amused smile sparks at the corners of her mouth.

"Your, what?" she says, as she leans forward and bats her eyelashes at him. Sean narrows his gaze. I can't tell if they're teasing each other or if they have a relationship that's in the weird middle spot where no one wants to be the first person to call it what it is—dating.

Sean continues to gaze at her without speaking. I shift in my seat and look over at Peter. He gives me a look that says he has no idea.

Avery smirks and makes the introduction for him. "I'm Avery Stanz, his favorite call girl." She winks at Sean at the same time my face flames red. For a second I think she's teasing him, but the look on his face says otherwise.

Sean leans back in his chair, and he shakes his head. He's smiling, but I can't tell if he wants to strangle her or hug her. "I spoke too slowly. Now you both know how fucked up things have gotten and why

I haven't left New York yet. I'm sure you noticed the pattern shift, Pete. Everyone else has." Sean's eyes shift back toward Avery as he's speaking. The look he gives her is so intense that I can't look.

Peter watches Sean but doesn't say anything. The silence drives me nuts, so I blurt it out. "For real? Like you sleep with men for money?"

Avery's perfectly pink lips switch from a coy, sexy grin to a big fat smile. She laughs and looks over at me like she didn't notice me before. "Ah, here we go. Sidney's my kind of girl—"

"I don't do girls," I squeak, which makes Avery start laughing. She lifts her napkin to her mouth to muffle the sound because it's way too loud for the restaurant. People look over at us. I'm pretty sure my face caught fire because there's no way blushing could possibly make it sting this bad, this long.

"Oh my God, she blushes, too!" Avery drops the napkin and grins at me.

Sean translates, "Avery blushes an abnormal amount for someone in her profession and has a tendency to say whatever random thought flies through her mind. She thinks you're her long-lost sister from the look on her face." Sean grimaces after I hear a scuffle under the table. I think she kicked Sean.

"Shut up! You'll scare her off," Avery teases.

I lean forward and raise my hand, like I'm in school. "Can we stop talking about me like I'm not here?"

Peter tries not to laugh and flashes his baby blues at me as he covers his mouth with his hand to hide the growing smile on his lips.

"Oh my God. I love her." Avery stands and smooths her dress before walking over to me. "You guys talk about boring man stuff. We're going to the bar to get better acquainted." Avery touches me lightly, but when I don't get up, she threads her arm through mine and pulls me.

"Um, I don't do girls."

"Yeah, I got that, sweetie." She's still laughing at me. "Come on. Let's leave the boys alone so they can talk."

Oh. Now I feel stupid—well, stupider. Avery holds on to me as we cross the room, arm in arm, toward the bar. An old guy nods at her, and I wonder if they know each other. A few male heads turn as we walk by. My dress is much more conservative than hers, so I assume they're looking at her. I'd die to have her body. It's all curves in all the right places.

She leans in, and says, "Walking like this puts ideas in people's minds. Those looks we're getting are for both of us. Wait until we sit down. Some hot guy will ask for your number within five minutes." She winks at me right when we get to the bar.

I'm insanely uncomfortable, but I try to relax. This chick is just a person with a weird job. She seems nice, really. I would have never thought she was a hooker if she didn't tell me. I press my lips together. I have no idea what to talk about. Avery chooses for me. "So you guys drove up from Texas?" The bartender hurries over and Avery orders two shots.

Nodding, I say, "Yeah, but I don't do shots."

She laughs. "Neither do I. I'll claw my tongue like a cat in a second. Watch and see."

I can't read this woman. I can't tell if she's pulling my leg or if she's for real. The bartender sets down two tiny cups of amber liquid. She plucks one from the bar. Just as I lift mine, she clinks them together and says, "Mazel tov. Here's to the fucked-up Ferro brothers." She knocks back the shot before I can speak, and then makes the funniest expressions I've ever seen. Apparently she wasn't lying about the not doing hard liquor thing.

I can't help but laugh. She's got her mouth hanging open and is fanning it frantically. Just as I'm about to do the shot, a man sits down next to me. "Hey, beautiful, can I buy you a drink?" I turn and look at him. Holy shit, he's hot. The guy looks like a *GQ* ad, complete with amazing eyes and sun-kissed skin.

I blink in shock and fail to respond. He looks over at Avery. "I'm sorry. Are you two together?"

Avery gives him a look with those dark eyes and leans into me as she places her hand on my arm. "Yes, and I'm buying her drinks tonight. Scat."

The man smiles at us with a look of sheer appreciation laced with lust. "My apologies. Enjoy your evening." He slips off the stool and takes the walk of shame out of the bar.

I gape at her. "Why'd you say that?"

"Because you think you're a fucking wallflower and you're not. Now you know. Hot guys want you, even in that frocky thing you're wearing." She taps the bar and nods at the bartender. He brings Avery another shot, but she doesn't drink it just yet.

"It's not a frock! I thought I looked cute." I look down at my dress. Is it that bad?

"You look like a schoolmarm. It's the classic don't-look-at-me long black dress. In Latin, it's called *guyus replantunus*." She grabs my long skirt and waves it back and forth. "What is this? A broomstick skirt? Don't they show off knees in Texas, or is that illegal?"

I glance at her skirt. It's not tight but it's much shorter. I can see her shapely thighs and so can every other person in the room. She notices me looking and smirks. "I don't do women, in case you're still nervous about that. Actually, I haven't been doing this very long, and Sean Ferro was my first client."

"No way, really?" My fingers tap the lip of the shot glass as we talk.

Avery nods. "How'd you land the brother?" She looks behind us. We can see the two of them from here. They're speaking with mirrored expressions. It's a little insane how much they look alike.

I smirk because it was so unlike me. "I walked up to him in a parking lot and offered to sleep with him. It was kind of random. I was trying something new." I can't look at her.

"Looks like it worked out."

"Actually, he threw me out that first night." Screw this. I'm doing the shot. I lift the glass to my lips and let the liquid flood my mouth, but it's too slow. It starts to burn before I manage to empty the glass.

Avery laughs. "Holy fuck, you're crazier than I am. Swallow it before it burns a hole in your face!" She's too loud. Everyone turns to look at us.

I feel too many eyes on the side of my face and panic. I can't swallow the liquor. It was too much and my eyes are burning like my brains are on fire. I start to squeal and fan my face, like that'll help. Avery yells at me to swallow it, but now I can't. I have too much liquid in my mouth and I'm pretty sure my tongue has flames shooting out the end.

I frantically look around, trying to figure out how to spit it out, but there is nowhere. *Way to be classy.* There's a couple of guys sitting a few stools over drinking. The one closest to her has a tall glass. Avery reaches for it, tosses the contents in the drain on the other side of the bar, and slams it down in front of me. I spit it out into the cup as fast as humanly possible while Avery laughs hysterically.

"Oh my God, you're just like me!"

I'm not sure about that, but I can't talk. I fan my open mouth as people stare at me with knowing expressions on their faces. Avery leans into me, laughing, and tells me not to scrape my tongue, since that will only make it worse. My eyes water and tears streak down my face. The bartender shoots Avery a look and puts down a glass of water in front of me. Avery reaches into her purse and slips him a big bill. All is forgiven, and he actually smiles at her.

"That was the funniest thing I've seen in an insanely long time." She hangs on my shoulder and then looks at me. Her little fingers dab away my tears without messing up my makeup. "There you go. Good as new."

"That was so disgusting. I can't believe I spewed." I start giggling and can't stop. Avery chortles with me. It feels like I've known her forever. It's really weird and not lost on me. I don't get along well with many people. I tap her arm a few times and manage to say, totally straight-faced, "That was evil. Really. Frock you."

Avery honks out a huge laugh and slaps her hands over her mouth. Frantic giggles burst forth from both of us and fill up the bar. I can't breathe, and I'm pretty close to falling off my stool. A guy tries to hit on us, but neither of us can stop laughing long enough to look at him. A second later, I feel his hand on my shoulder. The smile is torn off my face as I round on the person, ready to punch. I've already formed a fist when Avery touches my hand.

It's not a random guy. Sean is standing there looking much too serious. His deep blue eyes shift between Avery and me. "Ladies." He arches a dark brow at me like he disapproves. "Dinner is on the table." He extends his elbow to me. I hesitate because I don't want to take it. My skin is still covered in goose bumps from the first time he touched me.

Avery leans forward and pushes his arm away. "We'll be right there. Give us a sec." Sean looks annoyed, but walks away. His posture is so perfect. He carries himself differently than Peter, but their confident stride is the same. Avery pulls me out of my thoughts. "You okay?"

"Yeah, I'm fine." I'm not. I'm too jumpy for a normal person and she noticed.

Avery gives me a knowing look. "If you ever need somebody to talk to, I've been through hell and back. I know stuff, even if I seem like an idiot most of the time."

I appreciate the gesture, and smile at her. The look she gives me says she knows what happened on some level. I see it in her eyes.

I nod and tuck my hair behind my ear, breaking her gaze. "I might have a question or two for you, actually." I tell her what I'm thinking, and she answers my inquiries without judgment.

CHAPTER 17

"Peter tells me that you were his student." Sean gives me a sharp look that says I'm devoid of morals.

"Yeah, Peter was my boss, too." I poke around at my food.

Peter ordered for me while we were at the bar. The food is good, but it feels like I'm being judged and I hate that. Especially by him. Sean pisses me off. He has this superior thing going on, and I can't stand it when people think they're better than everyone else. Maybe I shouldn't say it, but I do. I place my fork down and look up at him. "Listen, if you want to throw stones, you probably shouldn't have bought your date."

"Oh, snap." Avery grins and lowers her gaze to her salad.

Sean's eyes bore into mine. I don't look down. He's a facsimile of Peter with harder edges. "You think I'm judging you?"

"Yes."

"I wasn't," he says, still staring at me like he has no manners at all.

"Then why'd you bring it up?"

Peter watches us but doesn't intervene. Instead he leans back in his chair and steeples his fingers, tapping them together lightly and looking at his brother.

"Because I thought it was interesting." Sean cuts his gaze over to his brother. "Is she always this adversarial?"

"Only when you piss her off." Peter smiles at me and resumes eating his dinner. His eyes flick up with amusement after he takes a bite.

"It was a rude question," I say, still glaring at him. Maybe I should let it go.

Sean straightens in his chair. "Very well. Then turnabout is fair play, so ask something of equal boorishness."

"Boorishness?"

"It means rude—"

"I know what it means. Fine, I have a question. Why do you keep calling Avery? Why not just date her like a normal person?"

Sean sounds completely dignified when he says, "Because I'm not a normal person."

I give him a face that says I think his answer is crap.

Avery leans forward and rests her elbow on the table as she gazes at him. "Sean, you told her to ask you. Tell her whatever you want." They are the weirdest couple I've ever seen. She's so light, and he's so dark. I wonder if there's more to both them. There has to be some common thread somewhere.

Sean leans back in his chair and looks me over. "I don't like you."

"I don't care." *Holy shit, that was blunt. Who the hell says stuff like that?* Peter is getting agitated, but I shake my head slightly. I don't need him to rescue me, not from this guy.

Sean makes a disgruntled sound at the back of his throat. "I asked her to be my mistress."

"How flattering." I glance at Avery and can tell my gut reaction is right—it's not flattering at all.

"Isn't it?" Sean's tone sounds sincere but he can't be.

I glance at Avery. "Is he serious?"

Avery nods. "One hundred percent." Her voice hitches slightly, like it bothers her that he didn't ask for more. I catch it and wonder if Sean knows. He doesn't seem to, but then again he seems to be acting assy on purpose.

"Well, good luck with that, Sean." I don't mean to, but I make a face as I look at Peter.

Sean doesn't let it slip by. "You think it's inappropriate? Really, after screwing your professor and superior, you really think you have the right to judge me?"

"Sean," Avery warns and glances at Peter.

"That's enough," Peter scolds. It silences Sean, but I stare burning holes into Sean's forehead. He glances up at me.

"You think I'm after his family's money, don't you? You think that I'm not good enough for him, that I'm some white-trash gold digger. Isn't that right?" My jaw tightens as I speak. I see it in his eyes before he has a chance to answer, so I cut him off. "I don't need his goddamn money. I can get by on my own. I always have, and I always will. You on the other hand will die miserable and alone. In the five seconds since I've met you, I could see that Avery deserves so much more, more than you could ever give her. You're chasing a dream. Wake up." I snap the last two words at him as my palms slap the table. The silverware shakes.

I glance over at Peter. "I'm sorry, Peter. I'm not sure why we came here tonight."

Peter exhales slowly and glances at Sean. There's a warning in his eyes. At first I think Peter's telling Sean to back off, but that isn't it.

Sean rolls his eyes, like this much drama gives him heartburn. He taps the butt of his knife on the table before lifting it and using it like a pointer, gesturing to his brother. "Because Peter wants me to come with the two of you."

CHAPTER 18

"Peter wants you to do what?" I swear to God the vulture must have eaten my brains while I was asleep last night, because there is no way in hell that Sean just said that. Peter didn't tell me what he wanted or why he needed Sean, but I don't like it, mostly because Sean hates my guts for no apparent reason. It's hard enough facing what I have to face. I don't want Sean there crushing me as well.

Peter leans forward and takes my hand. "It's just for a day or two. You don't even have to talk to him." Sean doesn't move, but the way he watches us says everything. He thinks that I'm bad news for his little brother. Sean's gaze returns to his plate. His lips part as he cuts through his steak. Peter turns abruptly and cuts off Sean before he can speak. "Shut up and eat your dinner."

Avery pokes her food and eats slowly. She didn't know their plan either based on the look on her face. "How long will you be gone?" It's a loaded question. Avery isn't asking for dates, although that's part of it. She's asking Sean something else. I wonder if he notices.

Sean's voice softens, but he doesn't look at her. "Only a couple of days."

She nods. "What about tonight? And tomorrow?"

"It's your decision," Sean answers, sounding like he couldn't care less.

Avery gently places her fork down, then puts her napkin on the table. She stands and smiles at Peter and me. "It was nice to meet you." She turns to Sean and gives him a look that could castrate another man. Her voice is cold and completely detached. "Do whatever you want."

Avery walks away, but I don't know why. It feels like they were having a private conversation even though it was in front of us. Sean said the wrong thing. He doesn't chase after her, and Avery doesn't slow down or look back. She knows Sean won't rush after her.

Awkward silence fills the table. Peter is leaning on one arm, watching his brother with a grin on his face. Sean lifts his dark gaze and notices Peter's amusement. "What?" Sean snaps.

"You like her, a lot."

"It's not your concern." Sean sips some of that disgusting amber liquid from his glass.

"Of course not. Just stating the obvious." Peter's gaze follows Avery. "It's interesting; that's all. The woman clearly brought you to your knees, but you're too proud to chase after her. Too bad she's used goods, huh?" Before I can scold Peter for saying such a thing, Sean bolts upright and grabs Peter by the throat. Sean hisses something, but Peter is laughing over the threats. Peter rips his brother's hands away and blurts out, "You are so fucked."

Everyone is looking at us. Sean sits down again as Peter continues to grin like it's funny. I kick Peter under the table, trying to make him stop. Sean is sending off the crazy vibe in massive waves and I don't want him to kill us in the parking lot.

Peter shakes his head and pushes his hair out of his eyes. "So you know?"

Sean works his jaw before taking a swig from his glass. "Of course I know."

"Does he know what?" I interrupt and look between them.

When Sean doesn't answer, Peter says in a playful tone, "He loves her."

"Then why'd you let her storm away?" Sean glares at me with venom in his eyes. He doesn't like this, but I have no idea what part he finds objectionable. Screw this. Avery was nice and this guy clearly needs a kick in the ass. "Do you need a textbook or something? Avery knew you wouldn't follow her when she walked away. She wanted you to say you wanted her. She wanted to go with you. What the hell are you sitting here for if you love her? How damaged are you?" I don't understand him at all. That cold confidence speckled across Sean's face is maddening, especially if he really loves her. Sean holds himself in check and buries every emotion that might play across his face.

Peter is nothing like Sean. They may look the same, but they're not. Peter still has a lightness about him. He jokes, smiles, and teases. Sean had all the light sucked out of him a long time ago. The man is a thunderstorm waiting to kill someone.

"Why should I go after her?" he asks callously. The way he sits in his seat and doesn't bother to look up at me says he could care less what I think, but then again, people like Sean don't waste words.

"What, do you need a lesson or something? If you love her, you can't let her think you don't care. And why the hell are you sharing her with other men? Or women or goats? Or whatever the hell she's doing? Why haven't you saved her yet? What are you waiting for, an invitation?"

Peter's gaze flicks between me and his brother. When Sean looks his way, Peter smiles pleasantly, like I didn't verbally bitchslap his brother. Sean asks Peter, "And your opinion is…?"

"My opinion is that the great Sean Ferro has fallen. You're a dick if you let her get away. She seems to tolerate you for whatever reason and you let her leave." Peter lifts the bread basket and tears off a piece of a roll, then pops it in his mouth. "No one tolerates you unless they're blood or paid."

"She's paid," Sean says in a clipped voice.

"It's more than that, blind boy. Open your eyes." How can he not see it?

Sean turns in his seat and looks at me. "You want Avery to come with us?"

I shrug and look at Peter. "It's not like I invited you. Oh, and shotgun. I'm not sitting next to the turkey."

Sean gapes at me. I feel his eyes on the side of my face. "What?" I don't offer clarification, although I feel bad for the turkey.

Sean looks over at his brother. Peter's beyond amused, wearing a huge grin that makes his eyes sparkle. "Oh, she's serious. She has a pet vulture that she seems to have named 'the turkey.' That isn't a very good name, Sidney. And, I'd like to add shotgun. That bastard will peck your eyes out if you drift off."

CHAPTER 19

Peter and I are in the elevator. We left Sean sitting at the table alone. That man worries me. I wonder if that's what's at the bottom of the cliff for Peter. When Peter first told me about Sean, he said his brother was messed up. I tighten my grip on his hand and lean into him. "Were you like that?"

"What, like Sean?" I nod. Knots tie up my stomach. I'm a little bit afraid of what Peter will say. We exit the elevator on our floor and walk down the hall. Peter shakes his head. "No, at least I don't think so.

Sean's not the kind of guy who wears his heart on his sleeve."

"That's an understatement. Damn, and I thought you were a head case." I realize what I've said after I say it and smile weird since I can't gather the words and swallow them back down.

Peter stops me before we get to the room. He grabs me by the waist and places a hand on either side of my head so that I lean my back against the wall. I look down at my dress, wondering if I really am wearing something that was made for old ladies. Broomstick skirts are for grannies with cankles. I don't remember why I bought this dress.

A smirk lights up Peter's face. He tucks a piece of hair behind my ear, saying, "You thought I was a head case? Me? You realize you're in this relationship, too, right?"

"Yeah, but me and you are equally nuts, where Sean is meganuts." I glance up at Peter. "He's a little freaky. Why did you want him to come?"

"Because he's a little freaky and I need his help. Dean won't mess with you after this. No one will." Peter kisses my forehead and takes my hand. We walk to the room in silence. I don't know what he intends to do about Dean. There's nothing to be done.

"Peter, what are you going to do?" I don't like the tone of his voice, but at the same time I love it. I hate that Dean did what he did and nothing happened to him. He turned my own damn family against me. I lost everything because of him.

When Peter doesn't say anything, I grab his shoulder and turn him around. Those vivid blue eyes look back at me. "Are you going to hurt him?"

"I'm going to make sure he doesn't hurt you anymore. Don't worry, Sidney. Go home, talk to your mother, and see if you can make peace with your family. That's what we came to do. Let me handle Sean and Dean."

"What about Sam?"

"What about him?"

"You sound like you're planning to do something." My gaze shifts between his eyes, looking for the truth. "Don't hurt Sam."

"Sam should have protected you."

"Sam's an asshole, I know that, but—"

Peter kisses the top of my head. "Calm down. I won't hurt him if he doesn't hurt you. If he stands there and does nothing again while Dean beats the shit out of you, then he'll have a problem."

"Sam wasn't there."

"Then there's nothing to worry about."

I nod slowly. Having someone looking out for me is different. I don't know what to do with the feelings that are rising up inside of me. Half of me says that I should be able to take care of myself, but the other part knows I need help. I morph into the timid girl I was when Dean hurt me the other night. She resurfaces no matter how far I've come. Sometimes I think my mind is going to snap, that I'll bear more grief and pain than I can tolerate. I hope to God that I never get pushed that far. It's extremely obvious that Sean was pushed past his breaking point. The idea of living in a broken mind, unable to mend, frightens me. I don't want that life.

Peter opens the door and we go into the room. It's small but posh. The bed looks like it is made out of fluffy white sheep. *Screw you, little lambs!* I can't wait to jump on it and all its cloudy goodness. The headboard is lined with fluffy white pillows. They look so soft and perfect.

Peter strips off his suit jacket and walks over to sit on the bed. I know his pattern by now. He'll undress and take a shower. Butterflies swirl in my stomach like a vortex. I place my hand on Peter's arm and stop him. "Wait a second." Peter looks back at me.

"What is it?"

"I…" *I suck at this. I'm mental. I love you. Go with I love you.* "I suck at this." Oh my God, my brain isn't listening to me. I look down, and when I glance up again, Peter has a curious expression on his face, no doubt brought about by my sudden timidity.

"I liked the way you held your own with Sean." I nod. I don't want to talk about Sean. I want to talk about Peter. I want to do something with Peter before I lose my nerve, but I don't know where to start. It's like he can sense it. Peter is all soft smiles and kind words. He tilts my chin up so I meet his gaze. "What are you thinking in that beautiful head of yours?"

"I want to try something with you, but I don't know how far I can go." I feel weird saying it. There's a rebellion going on in my mind, and it's been growing stronger each day. The more time I spend with Peter, the more I want to be with him, but it's not so simple. I expect to shut down when I try to press forward. The first time I tried to be with Peter was the furthest I'd gotten with anyone, and even then, I anticipated a major freak-out. Getting touched like that is like stroking his scar. There's no way to forget what happened to me. I just hope that one day I can push past it, that it will no longer dictate my life. I want this with Peter, but I don't know what it'll do to me. That thought alone is enough to make me chicken out, but I already threw the words out there. So I finish by asking, "Is that okay?"

"You don't ever have to ask me that, all right? We go and stop when and where you want. I won't push you at all, so you have to take the initiative here." He gives me that boyish smile I love so much.

I look away. Take the initiative? I can't do that. "I don't know how."

Peter reaches for me and then lifts my hands to his lips, kissing my fingertips. "Then tell me what you want, and I'll make it happen."

My heart flutters at his kisses, at his words. Maybe I can do this. I repeat the things Avery mentioned at the bar, the things that I could do that weren't sex— the things that would make me feel secure enough to be with Peter if I wanted to continue.

Peter's gaze darkens as I say the things one by one. "I can do that. That sounds perfect actually."

"It's not just teasing you to the point that you're going to hire a hooker?"

He laughs. "No, nothing could make me leave you. And being with you like that sounds perfect. I don't know if you noticed or not, but I'm a little gun-shy. I completely freaked out that first night we were having coffee and couldn't hide it. That's not gone. The emotions...it feels like betrayal, like cheating even though I know it's not. Slower is good for me, I promise."

I believe him. Every word he says pulls me closer and closer. Peter leans in and lightly brushes his lips against mine. "Wait right here. I'll be right back." I nod. My heart is pounding and I feel frantic, like I need to run. I shake out my arms and kick my legs, but it doesn't help so I crank it up a notch. Kicking my leg out hard behind me, I hold it and shake. The nervous energy is spent, so I do it again with the other leg. I turn around so I don't kick the dresser or punch the mirror and work my arms, too. I try to be quick, but apparently I take too long.

Peter sees me. "Are you doing the hokey pokey?" He's leaning in the bathroom doorway with his arms folded over his chest like he's been standing there the whole time. How come I never catch him doing anything dorky?

Feeling silly, I reply, "Maybe."

He grins and crosses the room. Water is running in the bathroom. Peter turns the lamps off so that only a streak of white light from the bath illuminates the room. Then he walks toward me slowly, outlined perfectly, and stops when we are toe to toe. Cupping my face, Peter pulls me into a kiss. It builds slowly, becoming deeper and stronger. When he backs away we're both breathless. Peter looks down at my black dress, then his eyes flick up to mine. He reaches for my hands and places them on his chest, leading me to the buttons.

Excitement shoots through me in a burst. I try not to smile, but I can't help it and the corners of my lips tip up. I remove his tie first and then start on the buttons. I slip them through the tiny holes one by one and push his shirtfront open. There's a white undershirt in the way. I glance down at his slacks, at the belt, and swallow hard. I reach for him, pulling on the belt and unfastening it. I don't think about the anxiety shooting through my veins or the way it's twisting my stomach into a pretzel. I've seen him naked before. This isn't new, but last time he stripped himself. Things change when I'm the one tugging his clothing off. Swallowing the apprehension, I unbutton his pants. I tug his shirt free and toss it on the' floor. Next, I slide my hands up over his skin and lift the undershirt over his head.

Peter is breathing hard, watching me. My hands trail over his chest, feeling the firm muscles beneath. I lean in slowly, trying not to think about what's next or how far I'll go, and press my lips to his chest. Avery told me not to think ahead, because it'll only freak me out. She's right about that. Moments of confidence pass as I do whatever I feel like doing. Peter sucks in a gasp of air as he threads his fingers through my hair when I slide my hands over his washboard stomach. When I pull away, I don't have the nerve to look at him, though I can feel his eyes on me.

The rise and fall of his chest is hypnotic. My eyes remain locked in place, as I inhale slowly. Peter's scent fills my head. It's become a familiar scent. It reminds me of smiles, sweat, and dancing. I splay my hands just above his heart and lean in close. Nothing distracts me. There are no distant thoughts lurking at the back of my mind. I feel safe. I know he won't hurt me. I know I can stop this right now and Peter will still love me.

Tension runs through his body, but it's not just desire. It's more than that. Part of Peter is holding back because he's also fearful, but for different reasons. It kills me to hear the pain in his voice when he talks about Gina. She changed him from a reckless boy into the unmarred version of the man standing in front of me. Sometimes a life can do that, change a person. I wonder what changes I'm bringing about in him and hope that they're good.

Peter's chest feels warm beneath my hands. His eyes on my face—I can feel them there caressing me—but I haven't looked up. When I do glance his way, all the air is knocked out of my lungs. Peter's gaze is deep and dark with traces of remorse. Last time we did anything like this, it didn't go anywhere. I slept next to him, and we literally went to sleep. Before that, he pushed me away. But now, I don't think he will. I think he wants more.

Remembering to breathe, I suck in a trembling breath and tuck a strand of hair behind my ear. "Is this what it's supposed to be like?"

His voice is deep and rich. "That depends. How do you feel?"

"Nervous, excited, happy…"

Peter smiles and nods. "When you find the right person, yeah—this is what it feels like." He takes a deep breath, trying to steady himself before taking my hand and placing it over his heart. It's beating fast and hard. "Do you feel that? We haven't even done anything yet and that's how I react to you."

I watch him for a moment, wondering if he's all right. A lazy smile lines Peter's lips, and his dark hair is hanging in his eyes. Lifting my hand, I touch the silky strands and push them back. Twin pools of pure azure are studying my face, learning the curves of my cheeks, and reading the shape of my lips. Peter stretches and lets out a nervous sigh as he runs his hands through his hair.

I react without thinking. I can tell Peter is emotionally scarred. It's not something I can change, but it feels like we both need this. If we can get past this part, we'll be better for it. Taking Peter's hands in mine, I pull him closer to the bathroom where the water is still running. The tub is going to overflow soon. My hands find his waist. I lean into him and slip my palms over the small of his back, while hooking my thumbs over the edge of his slacks. I slip them down and set them aside, then do the same for his socks after stripping each foot. Peter is wearing blue boxers that are the same color as his eyes. It makes me grin. I wonder if he did that on purpose.

When I finish, Peter is standing there wearing next to nothing and I'm still fully clothed. Peter agreed to let me do it this way—we both thought it would be better if I'm the one in control. I reach up behind me and feel the dress's zipper tab between my fingers. I pull it down slowly and let the clothing fall open in front. Peter's eyes watch the fabric slip away, revealing a black bra beneath. I shimmy the dress past my hips and let it fall to the floor. I bend over and slip off my stockings. I doubt that was suggestive, but when I stand up

Peter's expression says it was beyond sexy. His eyes greedily drink me in, but he doesn't come forward and touch me, not yet.

I'm a step away from him when I look down at my bra. The clasp is in the front. My heart is pounding like it's going to explode, but I unhook it and drop the material to the floor. Peter inhales shakily and blinks once—hard—like he's dreaming. My eyes fixate on his boxers and the obvious attraction. I swallow hard and step toward him. My nipples brush against his chest, and he sucks in. It's like that night in the restaurant, but more, oh my God, it's more.

I hold on to him tight before backing away and lowering my gaze to his boxers. Going down on my knees, I kneel in front of him and slip my fingers in his waistband. I remove the garment and gasp—I can't help it. He's perfect and right in front of me. My lips want to kiss him there, but I don't. I want things to move slowly. I don't want either of us to bolt.

After I stand and step back, I hook my thumbs in my matching panties and slide them past my hips. I kick them off, tossing them onto the pile of discarded clothing. Before I can think about being there naked and freak out, I take Peter's hand and lead him into the bathroom. The tub is full, and bubbles are pouring onto the floor. The room has the light scent of vanilla and lavender.

The tub is like a small pool, it's so large. We can both do the back float in there at the same time. It's nestled into the corner of the large room. Peter gets in first and the parts that make me nervous disappear beneath the waterline. I step in after him.

Avery said this would be easier than jumping straight into bed, and it gives us both a spot where we can put off being together if it needs to wait. It was good advice. My nerves disappear as soon as the warm water swallows my naughty parts. When I look at Peter, all I see are bare shoulders and a wicked grin. It makes me want to kiss those lips.

At first, I'm just sitting next to Peter, but that feels like we're waiting for a bus, so I ask, "Will you hold me?"

"Of course." He holds open his arms for me and I settle back into his chest, facing away from him. Peter wraps his arms around my waist, just under my breasts. The embrace feels good. I tilt my head back against his shoulder. "I like this."

"I'm glad. So do I."

"It's not too fast?"

Peter shakes his head. "No, it's perfect."

We stay like that for a little bit and then things change on their own. Sitting still isn't peaceful anymore. The urge to turn and face him is shooting through me and won't stop. I hand him soap, thinking it'll be a good distraction, but as Peter's hands move over my neck and arms, and down my back, I want more. That innocent little idea is making me hot enough to boil the water, and from the feel of it, Peter is turned on, too. I take the soap from him and set it aside before turning around to face him.

"Can I?" I don't really know what I'm asking for, but Peter nods. I place my hands on his shoulders and move in toward him. My pulse pounds harder and harder as I part my legs and feel the water shifting beneath me. I lower myself slowly on his lap, careful to keep his hard length below me. If Peter tilts his hips, we'll be doing way more than hugging.

I wrap my arms around him and press my naked body to his. I close my eyes and stay there listening to the sound of his heartbeat. Tingles fill me, making me hot in strange places. The desire to rub against him is consuming me. I try to brush it aside, but the urge won't die back. I lift my head and press my lips to the base of his neck. I give him one tiny kiss and then another. Peter's hands remain on my back. They don't dip too low or go places they shouldn't. I feel his grip tighten as the kisses continue. I slip my tongue up his neck, following instinct and whatever ideas tumble into my head.

Peter's beautiful lips are parted like he wants to say something. As he reaches for me, he pulls my lips down on his. My breasts slip against his chest as I try to get closer to him. Lust is coursing through me so loudly that I can't ignore it anymore. I want him. I need him. The kisses grow hotter as I fight the feelings I have, but they swallow me whole. I gasp and raise myself out of the water a little bit.

My voice is a whisper. "Can I?" My fingers tangle in Peter's dark hair. It curls around the nape of his neck, damp from the bath.

His eyes are locked on mine. He swallows hard but doesn't say yes. His hands are still on my bare skin, holding me there. There's a far-off look in his eye like he's somewhere else, but I know he's not. I hesitate. I don't want to push him if he's not ready. I can't imagine what's going through his head right now. "It's okay. We can wait."

Peter smiles at me. It's the warmest, most stunning smile I've ever seen on his face. His hands find my waist. "Make love to me, Sidney. I'm yours. I'll always be yours."

The pressure on my waist increases. I lean into him, sliding against his chest as our hips line up. I feel Peter beneath me as I slip down into the perfect place. Peter closes his eyes and moans my name. His hands push on my hips, tilting them, which makes the movement feel divine.

I no longer know what I'm doing. I have no plan and no intention of stopping. I do whatever feels right, whatever makes Peter moan and close his eyes. The look on his face is perfect—it's bliss, lust, and love all spilling together. I lift off of him again and again. Each time delicious heat builds inside of me. The rhythm of our bodies rocking together becomes faster and steadier. We both climb higher and higher, lost in lust. Just as I shatter, Peter finds his release and stills. I slip down against his chest and hold on tight.

After a few moments, things start to sink in. I made love to Peter. I had sex without freaking out. A soft smile spreads across my lips and I hug him harder.

CHAPTER 20

The next morning, I have a huge smile on my face that I can't hide. When I roll over and glance at Peter, he's already awake with a mirrored expression.

"How are you?" His head is still on the pillow with his lower body tangled in the sheets.

"Really good." I'm wearing my pajamas because I'm mental and can't sleep naked. I fight the urge to pull the blankets up to my chin. Part of my brain is squealing like a twelve-year-old girl, *I'm in bed with a hot guy!* I try to stop smiling, but I can't, so I tug the sheets up to cover my goofy grin.

Peter's hand juts out and stops me. "I don't think so. I want to see that satisfied smile on those lips." He stares at me for a beat and then brushes my hair out of my face. "God, you're beautiful."

That makes the smile worse, and I blush as more of last night comes back to me. Peter likes that. He holds me in his arms whispering sweet words in my ear until there's a knock at the door. I glance over at him, wondering who would bang on the door this early. It's barely sunrise.

Peter gets up, pulls on boxers, and pads across the room to the door. He looks out the peephole and sighs. "It's Sean." I yank the blankets over my head and hide. I hate Sean. No, I hate Dean; I detest Sean. I think. I might have to make a list or something.

Peter chuckles after seeing me duck below the bedding, and pulls the door open. I can hear their voices with the down blanket over my head. "Good morning, Pete. There's been a change in today's itinerary. We need to stop by

Mom's first. Jonathan did something and she's livid. I knew I shouldn't linger in the city. And, as much as I'd like to ride with you and Sidney, I'll take my bike. I'll see you there at lunch. Don't eat without me." There's a noise, like Sean slapped Peter on the arm in a manly embrace.

Peter says, "Afraid of the bird?"

"Where is the beast?"

"In the kennel downstairs. I had to pay them twice as much to take it," Peter explains.

There's a pause and Sean adds, "And you used your old name."

"Maybe." That makes me grin. Peter says it just the way I would have.

"You could have called me, you know," Sean says. "Disappearing like that had Mom more neurotic than normal. She made me track you down. I'll always find you, Peter. I did find you. I left you alone because I thought you were doing what you needed to do to get on with your life, but I have to ask you this—how much does this girl mean to you? Is she worth the risk?"

Peter's voice is stern. "I already answered that last night. Either you help me or you don't, but don't sit around questioning my motives. You already know my intentions. Leave it at that." Peter's voice drops to a hissing whisper. His tone is clipped and beyond annoyed. I don't know what they spoke about last night, but it's painfully clear that Sean doesn't like me at all.

"Fine. It's just odd timing, that's all. You finally get your head on straight and you fuck the first piece of ass that bats her eyes at you—" There's a loud crack as something slams into the open door.

I throw the blankets back and sit up to see what happened. Peter has Sean pressed into the wall and the two guys look like they're going to kill each other. Peter is hissing threats when I dart across the room. Sean replies, equally upset, but none of it makes sense to me.

I pull on Peter and say his name too many times to count. "Let him go, Peter. Stop it."

Peter steps back and flexes his hands several times. He paces in a swift circle, never taking his eyes off of Sean. Sean has a smug look on his face. "You're not thinking straight, Pete."

I'm livid. Sean can't come in here and do crap like this. Peter's been fine, but when Sean's added to the mix, Peter becomes enraged. I step up to Sean. "If he's not thinking straight, it's your fault, you callous bastard. Peter's been through enough. Help him or leave him alone. Stop antagonizing the crap out of him for no damn reason!" I'm not yelling. The voice coming out of my mouth is that low tone my mom used on me and Sam when we did something hideous.

Sean looks me over; his eyes notice the old clothing and my hair before glancing at the messy bedding. "There is a reason, miss." He rolls his eyes like he's forgotten my name and it doesn't matter. "You see, there are people that are toxic, people who poison others. I won't let you do that to him. Pete has been through enough, more than you could—"

Something inside my brain snaps. I'm close enough to do it, so I do. I shove both palms into Sean's chest and scream in his face before he can finish his sentence. "You think I haven't! You think this is a fucking game? Well, it's not! And yeah, I know what toxic people are, because I'm talking to one now!" I shove him again, but the bastard doesn't move. "I can't stand you."

"The feeling is mutual."

"Why? I mean, I have enough reasons to hate your guts, but you have nothing on me."

"You want more than Peter can give. You brought him here to ask me to—"

"Sean, stop talking!" Peter yells, so I can't hear his brother. "Stop! She didn't ask to come here. She didn't even know who the hell I was until the day we left. She doesn't want to be a Ferro. I'm lucky she didn't leave me when she found out, so cut the shit!"

At that moment, the elevator doors open down the hall and a security man is walking toward us swiftly. Sean's gaze cuts quickly to me. "You didn't know who he was?"

I glare at him and fold my arms over my chest. "Fuck you."

He smirks. "All in good time, dear."

"I swear to God, Sean—" Peter warns just as the guard is on us.

"Is there a problem here?" The man is older and looks really irritated. "Because I can make all sorts of problems if you guys don't have any, you get what I'm saying?" Peter and Sean just stand there. The guard looks at me. "You all right, miss?"

"No, this asshole is bothering us." I point at Sean. His eyes widen before they narrow like he hates me. I don't care. "Can you remove him?"

The guard says, "Come on," to Sean and tries to lead him away.

Sean glares at me, but there's a smirk on his lips, like he respects me for some twisted reason. "You mess with him and I'll break your goddamn neck."

"Mr. Ferro, please don't threaten the other guests—" the guard says, pulling Sean toward the door.

I talk over the guard and yell at Sean's back, "Go ahead and try!" By the time Sean is down the hall, I'm seething. My hands are clenched into fists at my sides and my jaw is locked. I slam the door and turn around. Peter is behind me, leaning against the wall with his arms folded across his chest. He watches me carefully.

"Are you trying to protect me from Sean?" Like I'd try to protect him from his own messed-up family? Peter is giving me a look that says he thinks so.

"Truth?" I ask, and he nods. "I don't know what the hell I'm doing. He makes me so angry and he doesn't listen to a damn thing I say. It's like he thinks he's so much better than me because he's a goddamn Ferro."

Peter gives me a crooked smile and pushes off the wall. "He thinks he's better than everyone because he's Sean. No one else in my family is like that, just him."

"No one else will be worried that I'm after your money?"

He shakes his head. "No, the gold diggers are after Jonathan now. Sean and I are seconds. Well, I am anyway. Sean made his own fortune doing God-knows-what. He's smart, ruthless, and ambitious, so of course he made his own fortune. I'm the middle brother—the guy with a broken heart who's all but broke."

"All but broke? I thought you had a trust fund?"

"I do. That's rich people speak for *Pete Ferro is a moron and walked away from a multibillion-dollar empire.* My trust fund is peanuts in comparison, but it's enough for me and you. I can't buy you a mansion—"

"I don't want a mansion. I just want you to be happy, Peter." My brains are starting to work again and I remember something Sean said. "Why did Sean think that I wanted something?"

"Sean always thinks everyone wants something. Just be glad he isn't riding with us. Come on. Let's get out of here. I'll grab you breakfast and we can head up to my mom's place and see what Jon did. It's not far from here. We can get to your parents' house by dinner." He pauses and shakes his head. "Maybe we should ditch Sean and head to your house now."

Peter is trying so hard to take care of me, and I adore him for it. For some reason the stuff with Sean feels like it's all or nothing. Peter wants his brother's help when I go home, and I want Dean to stay away from me. There has to be a reason why Sean is taking a detour to their mom's house, but I have no idea what it is. Either way, Peter needs Sean. "No, it's all right and we'd have to stop and grab lunch anyway. If you want to see Jon, we can go. Honestly, I'm not looking forward to what's waiting for me at home. Adding a few extra hours to the trip might help me deal with it a little bit better."

Peter presses his forehead to mine. "I'll help you through whatever lies ahead."

CHAPTER 21

The estate is breathtaking with manicured grounds spreading in every direction. An old stone mansion sits in the center of the property and sprawls as long as a city block. The house is nestled between the trees, and we have to take a long winding driveway to reach the front doors. I suppose it's so the house can't be seen from the road. I would have driven past it if Peter didn't tell me where to turn. I'm familiar with this part of Long Island, but I had no idea there were houses like this out here. I thought that most of the mansions were modern and on the south shore. Apparently there are rich people who prefer the other side of the island with the rocks and hills. The turkey notices that we stopped and cranes his neck to look out the window.

"What are we going to do with him?" I jab my thumb at the vulture in the backseat as I cut the engine.

Peter seems nervous, but he covers his apprehension quickly and walks around to open my door. We're in a circle drive in front of enormous wooden doors that form an arch at the top. It looks like a castle.

Okay, I'm just going to admit it. I had no idea this was Peter's life. He seems normal, and the people who live here can't possibly be average. Everything about the exterior of this house is larger than life. It makes me think of the inhabitants as royalty, not savvy businesspeople.

I glance at Peter. I have no idea how his family made money or where it came from. There are some people who were born with generations of wealth beneath them. That must be Peter's situation because I don't recall hearing anything specific. He's old money and he's in my crappy little car with a bird of prey in the backseat.

Nerves course through my body so fast that I can barely hold myself still. It's the Chihuahua effect. Those high-strung little dogs are always quivering. Peter offers his hand and pulls me out of the car. He leaves the door open, and the turkey hops out of the backseat and wanders off.

Peter grins at the bird. "Enjoy yourself," he says to the animal. A man appears out of nowhere and slips into my car. Peter left the keys in the ignition.

"Hey! What are you—" My voice is too high and panicky. The guy slams the door shut and starts to drive away. I try to lunge away from Peter, but he holds me back.

"Sidney, he works here. He's taking your car to the garages. You're not in the 'hood. Calm down." Peter has that knowing smirk on his face, like he realizes that I had every intention of running after my car. I nod and rub my hands over my arms.

"Sorry, I had no idea. I had no idea about any of this. What is your mother going to say about you and me? Should we even be here?"

Peter leans in and kisses the tip of my nose. "She'll think you're amazing, because you are. It's what you think of them that worries me." Before Peter can elaborate, a male voice hollers at him.

"Peter! Is that you? Holy shit!" The man is moving toward us from the side lawn. His walk turns into a sprint and then a full run. As he gets closer, I do a double take. Dark hair, bright blue eyes, and that same build as Peter and Sean. Unlike Sean or Peter, this guy is all smiles—full wattage with nothing held back. This man looks like he could easily run down the beach and never break a sweat. Every bit of him is toned, and running like that doesn't faze him at all. I expect him to stop when he's within a foot of us, but he doesn't. Peter gets steam plowed and pulled into a man hug. There's a lot of back slapping and a slew of questions.

"Where have you been? Are you all right? What are you doing here?" The guy steps back and looks Peter over. Joy is painted across his face, and he can't stop beaming. Peter has that half smirk he wears when he's excited and nervous. "Damn, it's good to see you, again!"

"You, too, Jonathan. You've grown up. I mean, look at you."

Jonathan grins, revealing a dimple that matches Peter's perfectly. His silky chestnut hair is a bit longer than Peter's and curls the slightest amount at the ends, giving him that sexy bedhead supermodels would kill for. The thing that's the most striking about him isn't the awesome hair, the chiseled features, or his radiant blue gaze—it's that smile. It's almost mocking and makes me want to talk to him more to find out what's caused that sexy smirk to appear on his beautiful face.

After a moment, Jonathan looks over at me. He brushes his hair out of his eyes and really sees me for the first time. He glances between Peter and me, quickly putting things together. "Where are my manners? Jonathan Ferro. I'm this guy's younger brother." He extends his hand, so I do the same, anticipating a firm shake, but Jonathan takes my palm and lifts it to his lips, and kisses the back of my hand. As I suck in a breath, my body goes rigid.

As I stand there in shock, thinking that rich people are weird, Peter laughs and slaps his brother away. "Cut it out, Jon! You're going to freak her out."

Jon grins at me, looking up from under dark lashes, and blushes slightly. "I'm just messing with you. So, Pete, who is this beautiful woman?" He tucks his hands under his arms after folding them against his chest. I glance between the two. They look so much alike, but the eyes are different. Although they are the same color, Jon's don't have that haunted look that Peter and Sean carry around.

Peter pulls me in front of him and wraps his arms around me, making it extremely clear that we are not friends, we're more than that. "This is Sidney Colleli. We're on our way to see her family in Jersey."

Jon blinks and the smile falls off his face. "Are you guys getting married or something? Because Mom won't give her blessing after—"

Peter cuts off his younger brother. "No, we're not engaged or anything like that." Peter sounds wistful, rather than horrified, which bodes well. He earned some points for not freaking out. "Actually, Sidney's mom is dying. We're meeting Sean here for lunch."

"Oh, I'm sorry, Sidney. That's rough." Jonathan takes a long, slow breath and looks at Peter. "Do you want your title back?"

Peter laughs like that's the funniest thing he's ever heard. "Hell no. You keep it."

"Did Mom know you were coming?"

Peter shakes his head. "No, I wasn't sure if I'd need to head this way, so I didn't say anything."

Jon gives his brother a delighted smile. "Well, you couldn't have picked a better day to stop for lunch. Dad has trophy number forty-seven here, and if Sean is coming—fireworks, bro. It'll be awesome! Come on."

I glance at Peter, wondering what Jon means, but the guy already took off. "Does he run everywhere?"

Peter nods. "Pretty much. That was my younger brother, the idiot—that's what my dad calls him."

"Nice." Actually, it's anything but nice.

"Yeah. Jon kind of earned a reputation for being, ah, how shall we say this, impulsive. If he sees something he wants, he gets it. There's no forethought at all or at least not any that we've seen. He still acts like a kid, living life fast and hard. He wants every beautiful woman that crosses his path. If I wasn't standing here, he would have hit on you with a dazzling array of flattery. He's good like that, which is why he keeps getting himself in trouble. I hoped Jon would settle down a little when I left and take on some responsibilities, but apparently not. Sean wants to slap some sense into him. Jon must have done something crazier than usual this time."

I'm still caught on the fact that the Ferro brothers' features are so strikingly similar. It's like the three of them stepped out of the same mold. "How old is Jon?

You guys look like triplets. It's kind of freaky."

Peter gives me a shy grin. "Yeah, we get that a lot. Sean is a little older, about a year, and Jon is about four years younger. He just started college when I left, so that makes him a junior next fall, assuming he went to class."

I smirk and look over at him as we walk toward that massive front door. Peter laces his fingers together with mine. I keep talking although nerves are filling my stomach. "I bet you always went to class, didn't you?"

"I'm the Goody Two-shoes of the family. Sean's the black sheep—or he sacrificed the black sheep when he sold his soul—and Jon's Jon. That pretty much sums it up."

"You're the straight-and-narrow brother? My God, who would have thought it?"

Peter laughs and squeezes my hand tight. "It's all in comparison, babe. Compared to Sean, I'm sane and civil. Compared to Jon I'm responsible and levelheaded. Compared to you, well, nothing compares to you so let's just say I'm lucky and leave it at that." He leans in and gives me a peck on the cheek.

CHAPTER 22

I'm sitting at a long table with light-colored linens. There's an enormous bouquet at the center with every shade of pink you can imagine. A long crystal stem holds the arrangement off the table so it doesn't block our line of sight. Brightly colored roses are the focal points with little crystals dripping over the sides—or maybe those are diamonds. The flatware is a matching shade of pale gold. I poke the knife with my finger, wondering how heavy it is.

Peter is seated across from me, and I'm right next to my favorite person again—Sean Ferro. As he lifts his napkin, Sean speaks softly so no one except me can hear his words. "Assessing whether or not it will fit in your purse?"

"Bite me."

"I'll have the guards strip-search you on the way out if any of the flatware goes missing."

What a dick. It's like he's trying to start a fight with me on purpose. I redirect my barb with a comment that should shut him up. "I see you messed things up with Avery. Smooth move, Ferro." I'm not calling him by his first name to his face. It feels too intimate, as if I actually like him or something.

I smile at Peter, who is glaring at Sean. Sean looks perfectly civil, but everyone knows it's a facade.

Sean's voice is flat. "She had to work."

I blink at him, shocked. Work means more clients, which means she's with another guy right now. Avery didn't want another guy; she wanted Sean. I shouldn't say it, but I can't help it. "What did you do?" I barely know Avery, but I feel so bad for her. Sean doesn't bother answering me, not that I thought he would. "She deserves better."

"Agreed." Sean's single word packs a punch, and I have no sharp retort. He doesn't look at me for the rest of the meal. The man is an enigma with a dash of psycho.

The Ferros have a tradition of requiring all the children to be seated first, prior to their parents. Peter told me that it's supposed to promote family unity or something like that. I'm surprised that Sean is here with us. He's been such a bastard that I can't imagine him bending to anyone's wishes. Jonathan leans forward with both his elbows on the table and looks completely bored. Maybe that kid is like a high-strung collie and prefers running over sitting. I wonder what his story is, what the guy did to piss off his entire family because Jon seems utterly calm considering his mother is going to throttle him at any moment. Then again, the despondent, emotionally disconnected thing seems to be a Ferro trait. All three of them have it to some extent, even Peter. As for Jon and Sean, that's where the similarities stop—well, except for the heartbreak stamp plastered across their foreheads. I wonder if Sean was given a warm greeting like Peter. If so, I didn't see it.

A few moments after we are seated, the patriarch enters the room. Mr. Ferro is well past his prime with silvery hair and a broad smile on his face. Fit isn't the right word to describe him, but he's not overweight either. To make matters more interesting, there's a woman on his arm who is close to my age. She's wearing a clingy silver dress that dips insanely low, showing off very ample cleavage. She smiles at the boys and waves the tips of her fingers at everyone except me.

Jonathan mirrors her little wave and winks, but the other guys ignore her as if she'll be gone in a week. I watch Jon straighten as his father walks into the room. At first I think it's out of respect, but the way Jon's eyes light up when he sees the mistress makes me wonder if the youngest Ferro is crazy enough to steal his father's girlfriend. Damn, and I thought my family is messed up. Where is Mrs. Ferro, and why does she put up with this crap? I'd like to ask that question, but I don't. Instead I sit still with a polite smile on my face and wonder why Peter came back here.

When Mr. Ferro sits down and spies Sean, he's surprised, but when he glances at Peter, he's stunned. His shocked features instantly morph into a huge smile. Mr. Ferro rises, steps away from Boobie Barbie, and rounds the table. Just as Peter stands up, Mr. Ferro gives him a bear hug similar to the one Jon gave earlier. "Pete! It's so good to see you!"

His dad shoots out more questions than Jon. Peter doesn't actually answer any of them. Instead he just smiles and nods. When his father glances at me, Peter takes that as his cue for the introduction.

"Dad, this is Sidney Colleli." Peter sweeps his hand in my direction. Sean completely ignores the introduction and keeps tapping away at the screen on his phone. He took it out as soon as he sat down. I glance at Jon quickly and get a flirtatious nod, complete with charming smile.

Mr. Ferro has an impressed look on his face. "So you're the woman who brought my son back to the land of the living?" He says it like I did something miraculous, like Peter was six feet under. Everyone is looking at me, Sean included.

Was Peter really that far gone? He didn't seem like it when I met him. I knew he was hurting, but the shock on everyone's faces to see Peter here and happy isn't lost on me. "He's a good man."

Sean sounds bored, like my words will make him fall over and go comatose. "Of course he is. He's a Ferro."

"And you!" Mr. Ferro gives Sean a severe look. "You missed your mother's birthday and every major holiday in between."

"My apologies," Sean replies, sounding completely apathetic. "I've been working." Sean is wearing a black sweater that looks to be made of silk and a pair of dark jeans. There are boots on his feet, and his hair is messier than usual. It's a strong contrast between the suit he wore last night.

His father is obviously irritated with Sean. He's about to say something when another voice cuts him off.

"Well, well. Both my prodigal sons have returned." An older woman with golden hair appears. It's cut short and tapered to her head in a fashionable style. The cold depths of her eyes make her appear soulless. There's no light on her face. Maybe she adopted Jonathan, because he's still smirking at the mistress like he plans on hitting on her after lunch.

Mrs. Ferro walks over to Peter slowly, assessing him. A cornflower-blue suit makes her appear regal and utterly proper.

Mr. Ferro's voice is civil, but there's a lot of tension, as if there are decades of unspoken words and worries. "Constance."

Mrs. Ferro inclines her head, but that's all. She walks past Peter without a second look and takes the seat at the head of the table. Mr. Ferro sits sandwiched between his wife and his arm candy. Every single one of them acts like this is totally normal.

My mother would have stabbed my dad with the salad fork if he cheated on her, never mind flaunting some bombshell and bringing her to lunch at our house. What the hell? I glance at Sean, but even he fails to comment on it. Oh my God, if this is normal, no wonder they're so messed up. The tension is so thick that it's choking me.

Mrs. Ferro looks up at me after placing her napkin on her lap. "Who are you?"

I glance at Peter. His mother is a scary woman. Her question sounds more like an invitation to leave. "I'm Peter's girlfriend." I can say that, right? It sounds stupid, but I suppose it's true.

Peter introduces me and is uncharacteristically quiet. His mother looks down her nose from across the table. "I suppose you're here to plead with me, then."

I glance at Peter and then Sean. Jon is smiling like everything is terribly exciting. I shake my head and correct her. "No, I'm not. Actually we're on our way to see my mother."

"Oh, so you're visiting other people's mothers, just not your own?" Her words are tack-sharp. Peter doesn't look up at her. God, no wonder why both Sean and Peter ran fast and far. The woman is horrible. She's an emotional black hole and anyone sitting next to her will be sucked dry. I glance at Mr. Ferro, wondering if that's why he's tethered to the hot chick.

I can't leave it alone. I know I should—Peter's mom has every right to be upset that her son ran off—but it's not like that. "My mother's dying, Mrs. Ferro. Peter wouldn't let me make the drive alone."

Mrs. Ferro stands. Without an explanation, she leaves the table and doesn't look back. Peter tells me that he'll be right back and follows after her.

Sean smirks. "Bravo. You pissed her off in less than five minutes. I don't think I've made her leave a room that quickly. And to think, I wasted all that time coming up with snarky remarks for number forty-seven down there. Apparently we just needed you."

"She said it like we're taking a joy ride to Atlantic City. There are other things going on." My throat is tight. I'm not explaining myself to him. "Excuse me." I get up and walk away from the table. I turn down a hallway and keep walking and have no idea where I'm going.

Footfalls race up behind me. Jonathan appears, breathing a little too hard as if he ran after me. "You saved my ass back there. She's been wanting to chew me out since I got home. Hey, are you okay?"

I nod, even though I'm not. By tonight, I'll be home arguing with my own mother. "I'm fine."

"Come on. Peter's this way." Jon explains how lunch probably looked really weird since his father brought his mistress. "He does it to piss Mom off, but the woman never reacts. It's like she's dead inside. Dad on the other hand needs a plaything. I'm not making excuses for him. I mean, if a guy gets married he should deal with it. That's why I'm never saying any vows like that." He physically shudders as if marriage were a fate worse than death. "It gets extra interesting around the holidays. I try to steer clear of this place, but I'm sure you heard since my actions precede me—I'm the reckless son." He looks over at me and grins. "Actually, I'm not reckless at all, but none of them can tell because they're all dead inside. I know you met Sean—case in point. The guy's a vampire, sucking out souls from California to New York Island." He grins and sings the last few words.

"I think vampires suck blood."

"Same difference. He's heartless and cold, plus the song makes him sound like a hippie vampire, which is amusing. There's some juxtaposition going on there." He's trying to make me smile, but my guts have already twisted into knots.

I offer a nervous smile as we turn down another corridor. "So your parents—they're not divorced?"

"The D word, no. Mom hasn't wanted one. She just tolerates whatever shit my dad pulls and doesn't say anything. Dad has more money if he stays with Mom. As long as the mistress doesn't care, things are pretty quiet. With Sean and Pete gone, there's not much to do around here."

"Stop spilling family business to a stranger, Jon." Sean is walking swiftly toward us.

"Sean, stop being an asshole. You've seen the way Pete looks at her—"

"I have. Go finish lunch." Sean stares down his brother, until Jon shakes his head and turns away.

I watch Jon walk down the hallway. His gait is so similar to Peter's, but different as well. Sean calls after him. "I heard what you did, by the way. I'll speak with you later."

Jon turns around with a huge smile on his face. "It's not open for discussion, bro. It's a done deal." Jon laughs and hurries off before Sean can say anything else.

His steely gaze cuts over to me. "I have what Peter needed. There's no point in lingering. Let's get going."

I wonder what they needed, but I don't ask. I just nod and walk with him to the front of the building. When we step outside, the turkey is waiting for me, perched on the bottom of the railing. My car has been pulled around and is in the center of the driveway.

"Are you throwing me out?"

Sean laughs lightly. "No, I'm making it easier for you to leave. There's a difference."

"No, there isn't, and you're an asshole."

"It's a matter of perspective. Get going. Peter and I will be along shortly."

He wants me to leave without Peter? Sean opens the driver's side door. The turkey jumps into the backseat and settles into his regular position. "Yeah, I'm not leaving without him."

Sean looks agitated. "Perhaps I could persuade you?"

"What the hell does that mean?"

"It means I can give you anything you could possibly want to drive away right now and never come back. Name your price." Sean's voice is utterly detached. He reaches into his back pocket and pulls out a checkbook. I say nothing. Sean scribbles something and rips out the check, handing it to me.

I unfold the check and blink twice at the number. Holy fuck, that's a lot of money. I could buy an island with this check and every little thing I could possibly want. All I have to do is get in the car and drive away. It's what Sean wants. I take the check and smile at him. I slip into the front seat of my car, and I'm sure Sean thinks I'm going to leave when I start the car.

"Good girl," Sean says, like he's pleased with me. God, he's such an arrogant prick. He steps up to the car to shut the door, but my foot is still hanging out. The lighter finally pops. I take it and step out of the car.

"Here's what I think of your offer." I touch the lighter to the corner of the check. I hoped it would catch fire and burn, but the thing barely makes the paper smoke. I press the lighter to the paper over and over again, but it doesn't burst into flames. It just makes little circles all over the check.

"Very cute. Go ahead and decorate the other side too so they match. The bank won't care."

The damn thing won't catch. I make an annoyed sound in the back of my throat and throw the lighter on the ground. Ripping the check into a million pieces I hiss horrible things at Sean and then throw the bits of paper in his face. "You don't own me. I can do whatever I want and I want Peter, so deal with it."

Sean flicks a piece of paper off his sweater but doesn't react. "I already wired the money into your account. The check was a showpiece. Get in your car and drive away."

I stare at him in shock. He can't do that! Can he? "What's wrong with you? Don't you want Peter to be happy?"

"Yes, I do, very much so. Based on everything he's told me, you have your own shit to deal with, and I don't want him to be any part of it. The best thing you can do for my brother is to get in your car, leave, and never look back.

"No matter what his last name is, Pete will always be a Ferro. He'll always have more shit than he can handle, and he really can't carry more. I'm telling you things that you already know. If money doesn't appeal to you, then maybe you shouldn't think about yourself at all.

"What's best for Peter? Dragging him with you is making him regress. He shouldn't be here. This place is toxic; our whole fucked-up family is poison. Peter knows that, but he came back for you—he's done everything for you, and you've led him straight into hell."

Sean's words are clipped. He delivers them with more passion than I would have thought possible. There's no doubt in my head that Sean is protecting his brother, that he knows better than anyone what kind of personal demons lurk at this house, in this place.

I want to say that I didn't know, that I'm not selfish, but I am. I slip into the car and let Sean close the door. The window is down. Sean leans in, saying, "You're doing the right thing."

I can't look at him. Gripping the wheel tightly, I hiss, "Take the money out of my account. If you leave a single penny, I'll come back and shove it up your ass."

Sean's lips twitch like he wants to smile. "Very well. By the time you're home, the funds will be gone."

Gone. The word rings in my ears. Peter will be gone as well. No doubt Sean will tell him something that will keep him from looking for me. I pull away slowly with my heart in my mouth. I had no idea what Peter went through, and bringing him back up here was the worst thing I could have done.

CHAPTER 23

I pull up to my childhood home after dark. It looks just the way I remember it—a big grassy lawn and gardens overflowing with flowers. I thought I'd have a house like this one day. Now I don't know what I'll have.

My phone has been silent since I left the Ferro mansion. I thought Peter would call me. I thought he'd come after me. I can't stand the thought of not seeing him again. I wonder what Sean told him and can't help but wonder where he is now and what he's doing.

I turn off the engine and open the door. Me and the turkey walk up the center sidewalk to the house. I ring the bell. I don't live here anymore. This isn't my home, and these people are strangers to me. My father opens the door wearing his normal nighttime garb—jeans and an old T-shirt. He has a bag of chips in one hand. He doesn't really look up until I speak.

"Hey, Dad."

Recognition shoots across his face at the same time he glances up. He stares at me like I'm a ghost. "Sidney." Dad doesn't say anything else. I can tell that there's a battle going on inside his mind. He's happy to see me but betrayed that I left. Awkwardness consumes me. I know leaving was the right thing to do, but still—I feel sorry that I caused them pain.

"Sam told me Mom's sick." He nods and opens the door to let me in.

"Yeah, she is. Things have been rough. She's been asking for you."

I nod and step inside. The house is filled with people, family, neighbors, and people from the past. Most of them glare at me. They don't know what happened, they just know that I ran off and broke my parents' hearts. They don't temper their disgust as Dad leads me inside.

"My baby came home! We're together again." He pinches my cheek so hard that it hurts. I smile at him and try not to pull away. His emotions flip, like he decided to let it go. Dad's all smiles and walking around showing me off the way he used to. He tells people that already know me that I'm his daughter, that his little girl came home. He's so excited to see me. He doesn't ask where I've been or why I didn't tell him.

Tears sting my eyes, but I blink them back. Leaving like that hurt him terribly. I can see it on their faces, and hear it in his voice. Dad sounds proud of me, which totally kills me. I left with good reason. I left because no one believed me. I left because they liked Dean more than me.

Dad circles me through the room, laughing loudly and beaming. I'm polite and smile even though I can tell that no one wants me here. That's when I see Sam leaning against the railing that goes upstairs to the bedrooms. His arms are folded across his chest. He glances behind me looking for Peter, but Peter is gone.

Sam steps toward us. "I told you I'd find her and bring her back. It's good to see you, sis." Sam leans in and gives me a quick hug. Everyone thinks he's wonderful, that he brought his wayward sister home. If they cheer, I won't be able to take it.

I look back at my dad. "What's going on with Mom? Can I see her?"

Dad takes my hand and pulls me into the kitchen. There are fewer people in this room. My aunt is making something on the stove. There are countless dishes covered in aluminum foil on the kitchen table. Mom's kiss the cook collection is still on display in this room. Everywhere I turn, there's another plaque or doll or apron that says KISS THE COOK.

Dad walks to the other end of the dining room and pulls out a chair for me. "Have you eaten? Beth, make her a plate."

I wave at Aunt Beth and say no, but they both ignore me. A moment later Aunt Beth sets down a paper plate over flowing with food in front of me. "Eat. You're too skinny." She gives me a look of disapproval and turns back to the stove.

"Dad, what's wrong with Mom?"

"She's got the cancer, baby girl. It snuck up on us. One day she was fine, and then she wasn't. We did chemo for a while, but it's too far gone. She already lived longer than they expected." He says the words stoically like he's said them a million times before.

"Why isn't she in the hospital?"

"You know your mother. She wanted to be home. We have everything she needs here. The only thing we were missing was you. She'll be happy to see you."

I nod slowly, letting everything sink in. I knew Sam said she was dying, but I didn't realize she was that far gone. My stomach sours. I dart out of my chair and race to the bathroom and dry heave until my brow is covered in sweat. Everything crashes into me in merciless waves. Remorse so deep that I can't fathom the pain, the lost time, the hatred and the fact that I didn't forgive her blast into me. In the back of my mind I always thought there'd be time to patch things up. It wasn't a conscious thought, but it was there.

Now, there is no time. I lost that chance and I'll never get it back.

CHAPTER 24

I'm numb inside and out, staring at nothing. A few hours have passed since I got home, and it's too much. My emotions overloaded and shorted out. The only good thing that's happened is that Dean hasn't shown up.

Sam finds me sitting outside alone. "Hey, Sid."

I take a sip of my soda. My stomach is still queasy. It's late. Most of the people in my house left. They'll come back every day until Mom passes away, bringing food and keeping my father company.

"I wanted to say sorry for the way things happened in Texas. I should have known you'd come back. I was worried about Dad—about what would happen to him if you didn't get up to say good-bye. He's been smiling too much lately, like he's losing his mind. Every day Mom slips further away. She wakes less and barely talks anymore. The one thing he wanted to give her before she dies is you.

"Anyway, I'm sorry. I handled it wrong and I shouldn't have brought Dean."

My brother rarely apologizes. My eyes are strained, so when I glance at him it makes my head ache. "Where is he, anyway?" I didn't see him inside and the thought of bumping into him at any moment has me on edge.

Sam looks at me like I'm making no sense. "Where is who? Dean?" I nod. "He doesn't come around anymore. Actually, after you left, Ma told Dean she'd bury him in the garden and use the frying pan she killed him with as his headstone. It was kind of intense."

I stare at him in shock. All this time I thought Dean was in my house with my family. I left because they believed him over me. Sam doesn't realize the weight of his words. He may be my twin but there's no crosslink between us. Empathy doesn't flow through some twin-type bond.

Sam looks over at me with a quizzical look on his face. "What?"

"Do you know why?"

Sam shrugs. "No idea. She lost it when you left. Maybe she just took it out on Dean. I don't know."

"But you still hung around him?"

"Yeah, he didn't do anything. He's a good guy, Sid."

I'm not having this conversation with him, so I don't answer. I resume my blank stare until Sam gets up and walks away. Dean's his best friend and always has been. It makes me wonder if Sam cares about me at all. Sometimes I think he must, but when he says things like that—I don't know anymore.

My dad steps outside and calls my name. It rekindles memories of playing outside well past dark and my dad standing at the door and calling us in. On warm nights like this my mom would make fudge, so being called in wasn't so bad. I've always had a horrible sweet tooth.

"Coming," I say and get off the bench. I've been outside thinking, wondering if I was right or wrong, and waiting for my mother to wake up. They told me that as her pain medicine wears off, she wakes up. There are so many things to say to her, but I haven't settled on anything yet.

"She's awake and asking for you." Dad smiles at me sadly. "I told her you were here and she smiled. She hasn't smiled in ages, Sid. Go on up."

Before I walk away, I throw my arms around him. Dad hugs me back and then shoos me, telling me to get up there. I climb the stairs and head toward my parents' bedroom. I ran down these halls as child. If a nightmare woke me, I'd run into their room so they'd protect me. But now everything is flipped around. My mom is being destroyed by her own body and no one can save her.

I stop in front of the door and reach for the knob, ignoring the churning in my stomach. My mother is awake, maybe for the last time. I need to say what I came here to say.

I walk into her old bedroom, but it doesn't look the same. There's a hospital bed with IV bags dripping from above her. Mom is lying back with her eyelids heavy. A thin blue blanket covers her legs and is pulled up to her chest, but her arms are on top. As I get closer I can see what the cancer has done to her, how it's aged her dramatically. She looks old and frail. Her once-vibrant face is ashen and hollowed. The dark hair that flowed past her shoulders is gone. People used to say we look alike. The resemblance is almost gone.

She doesn't see me. I press my lips together and step closer. "Mom?"

My mother's been staring straight ahead, but when she hears my voice, her eyes move, looking for me. I step into her line of sight, and a painful smile crosses her face. It's so light and fades quickly. "Sidney. You came home."

She lifts her fingers like she's reaching for me. I take her hand. "I'm home,

Mom." My throat grows so tight that I can't speak. My vision blurs with tears.

Her voice is so weak—barely a whisper—but she speaks to me. She tells me about her gardens and asks if the bulbs are up. It's long past frost, but she doesn't seem to realize that. I listen to her voice and curse myself for not coming home sooner. I avoided this because I thought there was nothing left here. I didn't know what happened after I'd gone, I didn't know she turned on Dean.

I kneel next to her bed and talk about anything and everything until it's time for her medicine. The conversation drifts to Peter.

"Do you love him?" I nod slowly. "Then don't let him go." She coughs and her body stiffens from the pain. I wish this wasn't happening, but I can't stop it. No one can. I'm going to lose her for good.

"Do you want me to get help?"

"No." She grips my hand harder. "I need to say something. After you left, I found your books. I read them. I wanted to know what I did that was so horrible that you'd vanish like that." She's so weak.

Her words come out in shallow puffs of air like she can't breathe.

"You read my journals?" I had several diaries when I lived here. The night I took off, I left them behind. There was no way to sneak out and take everything with me.

She nods slightly. "I wanted to fix it, but by then it was too late. I didn't know. I couldn't see it. There's no reason to forgive me, and I can't ask you for that. I wanted to tell you that I'm sorry I drove you away, so sorry, honey."

"You believe me?" My voice cracks with shock. Regret floods my chest, drowning me in remorse.

"Yes, but I'm too late. I wish I—" Her voice abruptly stops as she tenses in pain. When it passes, she manages to say, "I'm sorry." She mumbles the words as her eyes close. The grip on my hand loosens. She's barely breathing.

"You're not too late, Mom. I love you so much. I'm so sorry." My voice shakes as I say the words, and in the back of my mind, I know that I won't hear her voice again. There will be no more conversations, no more laughter or tears. This is it.

I return to my swing and wait out the night.

Just before sunrise I hear it—my father's voice. He wails, and something smashes to the floor inside the house. I sit there unable to think. Shock washes over me again and again. My senses deactivate and die within me. Somehow I move from the swing out back to the staircase where I see my father weeping. I sit next to him. Neither of us speaks. After a few minutes he takes a deep breath and wipes the tears away. He grips my shoulder firmly and pulls me against him.

Sam is standing at the bottom of the stairs, looking up at us with his shiny face ghostly white. For a minute, Sam forgets everything else and climbs the stairs to sit with us.

CHAPTER 25

I thought I mourned my mother, but I didn't, not like this. I've spent most of the day on the back swing staring at nothing. Aunt Beth tried to move me and shoved several plates of food in my hands. I didn't eat any of them. When I put them on the ground, my turkey wandered over and found me. He ate all the food and tried to eat the plate, too.

I grab the plate quickly and put it out of his reach. "I need to get you to a vet so you can fly again. Walking must suck. Once we get you fixed up, I bet you'll head over to the Turnpike to hang with the other vultures." Not that I've ever seen any over there.

Aunt Beth calls me from the back of the house. I make the bird scat. Aunt Beth already threatened to stuff him once today. She's been crying and cooking nonstop along with the other women in my family—well, all of them except me. For the most part, they've left me alone.

"Sidney, we're out of flour," she explains, dusting off her hands on the apron my mother wore so many times. I glance at her shoes. They're white like she dropped the bag. Flour clings to her pants. She nearly falls to pieces when she tries to explain what happened.

I smile at her to stop the tears, "I'm happy to get more, Aunt Beth. Do you want anything else while I'm there?"

"No, hon, just the bag of flour. We're trying to finish everything up for tomorrow." She wipes her hands on the apron and then pulls me into a hug. "I'm glad you're back."

I smile and nod. It's what I do when people say that, partly because I don't know what else to say, but also because I'm not staying. I never intended to stay here. I came home to bury my mother. After that, I'm heading back to Texas. I haven't told anyone yet. I think it'll kill my father, but I can't stay here. Regret is strangling me, and the longer I stay, the worse it gets.

Aunt Beth walks me into the kitchen. "Oh, take my van. I'm blocking you in." She tosses me her keys. I catch them and head out.

Aunt Beth has three little girls and a minivan that smells like SweeTarts. I drive to the grocery store a few blocks away, hoping that I won't run into anyone I know. I park her van off by itself, because she'll go batshit crazy if someone dings the doors, before heading into the store. I find what she wanted and grab a few other items before heading out. As I'm loading the last bag into the back of the van, the hairs on my neck prickle. I turn abruptly, expecting to see someone watching me, but no one is there.

Spooked, I climb into the van and drive home thinking there's an ax murderer hiding under the row of seats. I keep glancing back, but no one is there. Still the feeling of being watched doesn't fade.

When I arrive at the house, Aunt Beth runs out to grab the bags and disappears inside. I close the tailgate and turn around. Dean is standing right in front of me. Our bodies brush together, and when I go to step out of the way, Dean holds on to my wrist.

"Wait up. I've been trying to talk to you."

"I have nothing to say to you." I yank my hand back and turn away, ready to go inside.

"I'm sorry about your mom."

I hate him. I hate that he says it, that he thinks he has the right to be here. Turning slowly I glare with every malicious thought in my head clearly visible on my face. They start to twist inside my mind. "Go to hell."

Dean smiles, like it's funny. "I love this new you. The backbone is very becoming, Sidney. It makes your breasts seem larger than they are. Did your new boyfriend teach you to stand like that?"

Anger has been building inside of me, and when he mentions Peter, I can barely hold on to my temper. I don't answer. Instead, I listen to the pacifist side of my brain that tells me to walk away.

"Seriously? I come over to give you my condolences and you don't invite me in? What the fuck, Sid?"

"My mother threatened to bury you in the garden. You are not welcome in this house."

He has the audacity to laugh. "Yeah, I remember that. Apparently she believed you just a little too late. Life's cruel, isn't it? You didn't come home for all that time because she didn't believe you, but it turns out she really did. Such a waste." He tuts like the entire situation was menial, like it didn't matter at all. Fury races through my veins so fast that I want to crush him. I want to make him stop talking and hurt him as much as he's hurt me. I can't let the thought slip away. It builds bigger and brighter inside of me as Dean stands there like I'm pathetic.

Dean notices the change, but he doesn't know how deep the thread of insanity goes. He comes up behind me and slips his hand around my waist gently, like we're lovers. "How about we do things the way we used to. I have the same knife in my pocket. You feel it, don't you baby?" He presses himself to my leg so that I feel how aroused he is along with the knife in his pocket.

A twisted thought forms in my mind and I can't let go of it. It pulls me along, building quickly, becoming darker as it grows. I say no and try to turn away, but I know what he wants. He likes the fight, he likes me afraid. I play the part and Dean holds me tight. I let him drag me to his van this time. He pushes me against the side door and presses his body to mine. "You know you want it."

"Then let's go." I stare into his face without batting an eye. I mean every word I say. I want him alone. Now.

Dean's expression changes. Lust fills his eyes as he grinds his hips into mine. The movement makes me want to vomit and crawl back inside myself, but I don't. I remember the flashes of silver. I remember the pain, but most of all I still feel the remorse of losing my mother with vivid intensity and it's all his fault. Dean did this to me, to her. He stole everything from me.

The back of my neck is still prickled like someone is watching. I glance around quickly, but see no one. The street is empty and dark save for a telephone pole across the street and its yellow bulb. I suppose that it's my reaction to Dean; after all, being alone with him last time ruined me. My body remembers every last detail, but instead of feeling it rushing back, I feel nothing. It's like something inside my head stopped working. That rational part of my mind broke loose and rolled away. The only thing left is this thought that continues to grow darker and darker.

I slip into his van and Dean takes off. As he drives, he reaches over and places his hand between my thighs. All the blood obviously left his head because he doesn't notice the way I stare, the way I respond to his touch like it isn't even there. The void fills me, consuming my thoughts and pushing back any semblance of logic that tries to break forth. My mother is dead and the man sitting next to me destroyed any relationship I had with her. I could have come home. I would have come back had I known. The silent rage boils inside of me. Fragmented thoughts fly through my mind like a witch caught in cyclone. They're there and then gone in a flash. Consequences don't matter; nothing matters now. I've lost everything. My soul crawled up inside my body and died.

Dean pulls off the road and into a dark parking lot. At the very back is an old playground that's abandoned for the most part, and it looks exactly the way I remember. The night air is sticky and practically clings to me as I walk to our spot with Dean trailing behind me. It's the place he first kissed me before his kisses turned into something else. There's a concrete wall blocking the view from the parking lot. We're alone, surrounded by tall, dark trees and inky shadows.

As we duck behind the wall, Dean gropes me, pressing his hand under my shirt, and squeezing my breasts hard. He's greedy and I don't want him touching me, but I can't reach it—not yet. My heart pounds harder. I'm fighting to stay alert, but my mind is shutting down, falling into the terror of the memories that are burned into my brain. The memories rise up like corpses and demand my attention, but I don't give in to them.

Dean made me the way I am, what I am. I steel my reaction and cage my mind. I brought him here this time, not the other way around. I'll make sure he never forgets me the same way I'll never forget him, except this time I won't be a conquest. I stare blankly as Dean presses me against the wall. The concrete bites my elbows. Dean's hands are everywhere—on my waist, under my shirt, on my neck. The tip of his finger traces the scar below my necklace, flaring the scene to life in my mind. The old emotions splash over my mind, dousing me, and roll right off. I'm uncharacteristically still and utterly quiet, but he doesn't notice. He's saying things to me that are repulsive. Breathing hard, Dean presses me hard against the wall and grinds his hips against me, thrusting at me from behind his jeans. "I know how much you want my cock, Sid, and I'm going to give it to you—over and over again—until you beg me to stop. You like it this way; I know you do. Tell me, baby. Tell me how bad you want to suck it."

Dean's so strong. I can barely move as it is and once his pants come off, he'll do everything he said and then some. I can't wait anymore. I press my chest into his hands and reach down and slip my hand into his pocket. Dean makes a surprised sound, like he never thought I'd grab him like that. Touching his junk was an accident, and it masked what I was really after—his knife. My fingers wrap around the hilt and I take it from his pocket.

I step back and open the blade. "Remember this?" I flick it close to his face.

Dean's eyes widen and he tries to step back and comes up against the wall. There's nowhere to go. "Yeah, you want me to use it on you?"

I laugh, but there's no joy in it. "I remember all the times you did use it on me, all the things you did. I have so many scars from you that I can't think straight. No one saved me from you, and yet, here you are on the day my mother died, telling me that it's my own damn fault that I got raped, and that it was my fault that she never believed me.

"Oh wait, she did believe me—and you knew—and it's funny. Like ha-ha funny, like tragically ironic." I touch the knife to his throat as I speak, pressing the tip into his neck deeper and deeper. The last string that was holding me together has come undone, and it's blowing in the wind. No one will save me. It's like last time, and I won't have this man waiting for me in the shadows anymore.

Dean is swearing at me, threatening all kinds of things, but he can't move with the knife where it is without slitting his throat. I twist the point and watch a bead of red drip down his neck. My eyes flick to his. I feel the tension in my arm, the need to release the energy and fear, inside of me.

That's when I hear his voice. It moves through the shadows toward me. At first I think I'm hallucinating, then I actually see Peter. His dark hair hangs in his eyes and his face is lowered. He kicks a stone as he speaks. "As much as I think you should flinch and cut his throat, I know you. I know what will happen after you do, when it's over." Peter comes closer.

I can't move. I grip the knife tighter, thinking that Peter will try to take it away. I don't wonder why he's here or how he found me. I see flashes of silver and think the blade is on me. I act like I'm the one being attacked and I can't stop. I don't want to stop. "He used this on me, this same blade. He scarred me inside and out."

"I know he did." Peter is next to me, but he doesn't touch my arm. He watches me from under those dark lashes. "So what are you waiting for?"

"What the fuck, man?" Dean looks horrified. I twist the blade again, and Dean tenses, trying to push his body into the wall. I watch as the cut deepens, but it does nothing to make me feel better.

"When this is over," Peter asks, "what will you do? After all the blood has drained from his body, after he dies in front of your eyes, what will you do?"

The sound of my breath fills my head. I feel like I'm in control, but I'm not. I can't think; I can't blink. I don't know the answer to Peter's question, but I can't drop my arm. I'm locked in place, staring down the man who ruined my life.

"I know the name of the man who killed Gina. I know where he lives and I know exactly what I'd do to him. It would give me a great amount of pleasure to watch the light go out of his eyes."

"So why haven't you done something about it?"

"Because I already did. I once stood where you are now, but I didn't stop. I have to tell you that doing this will keep you trapped in your past for the rest of your life. This man will have ruined you in every way possible, and day in and day out you will remember that. Even after he's dead, he will haunt you. If you shove that knife into his throat and end his miserable life, he wins. He'll own you until you take your last breath. Is that what you want?"

His words hit me hard. A slew of emotions are twisting deep inside of me, trying to break out of the box I shoved them into. "I have to end this. I can't have him—" Peter's breath is on my neck. His hand is next to me and slowly slips over my arm.

"Then let me do it. Let me take care of this for you. You'll never see him again. I promise. Give me the knife." Peter slips his hand over mine as he speaks and closes his palm over mine. He pulls back slightly and the knife moves off of Dean's neck. He inhales sharply.

Peter holds me in his arms and kisses my face while keeping the knife blade accessible. The box cracks open, and emotions violently slam into me, so hard that I'm shaking. "I'm sorry, Peter."

Dean chokes and presses his fingers to his neck. They come away covered in blood. He starts yelling, "You crazy bitch, I'm going to make you—"

Peter's jaw tenses before he does it. His fist flies up and punches Dean so hard that he doubles over gasping for air. Peter releases me and slams his other fist into Dean's gut. Then he crashes a fist into Dean's back. The punches land harder and harder until Dean is on his knees and there's blood seeping into his shirt.

"Enough," a voice says and Sean appears. His hand is in his pocket. Sean's eyes flick to me, and he nods, like he's giving me his approval or something.

Peter is breathless. He wipes the sweat off his brow and says, "Tell him what he has to look forward to if he messes with Sidney again. Make sure he knows exactly what I mean." Peter's tension is palpable. Every last bit of him is strung like he's going to snap.

Everything happens so quickly. It feels like I'm in a daze and I can't do anything but blink. When did I become like this? What would push me so far that I'd actually hurt someone? Part of me is disgusted, but the other half is so damaged that I hope Sean scares the crap out of Dean. I want that man to hurt for everything he did to me—for everything he took away. That bastard stole my life, and I almost lost it completely. If Peter hadn't come when he did…

A shiver rakes through me, and reality catches up with my brain. A thin layer of sweat coats my skin. My face is so damn hot, but my arms are frozen. Before I can think, I'm forced to bend at the waist as my body tries to expel the contents of my stomach, but there isn't anything there, so I dry heave. Peter holds my back and speaks softly to me. His words float by my ears, but I don't understand him. I almost killed Dean. The thought hits me hard, and I can't stop shaking.

"I'll take care of this. Get her out of here." Sean grabs Dean by the neck and drags him into the woods. Panic shoots through me. I can't be responsible for this. Evil people are made by decisions like this. I can't allow it, no matter how far gone I was.

"Wait," I choke out, but Sean doesn't stop. Peter pulls me away, and I have to fight the urge to look back. "You can't kill him. You can't!"

"He won't kill the asshole. I would have if I'd come alone. That's why Sean insisted on being here today, now. He knows me better than I'd like to admit. Sean's just reminding that piece of shit that bad deeds don't go unpunished. Sean's a little more emotionally detached than I am. I'd kill him without meaning to." He looks at his hands like this is something he knows about himself, like he's killed before.

Sobs bubble up my throat, and I shiver. I shake my head and wrap my arms around my middle. Peter walks me over to a black sports car. It's Sean's, and the motorcycle is also Sean's. I slip into the seat and let fear strangle me into silence.

CHAPTER 26

The following day Peter stands next to me as I place a rose on my mother's casket. We stay until everyone else has gone. Sam sits on one side of me and my father on the other. Dad stares blankly. He hasn't cried since the morning she died. He smiles at me when he sees me and says I look like her. His words haunt me. Every time I look in a mirror to brush my hair or make sure I haven't smeared makeup all over my face from crying, I see my mother's face. There are pictures of her all over the house. The ones where she's my age rattle me the most. I have no idea what her life was like. I went from being a child to being an adult and left without ever really knowing who she was.

I think about Mom often and wish I'd had more courage to come back sooner, but looking backward doesn't help me move forward. Peter keeps telling me that. Mourning the dead is needed. Sobbing is needed, but there's a point when tears become smiles and the memories aren't filled with pain. I hope that day comes soon, but so far it hasn't.

We drive back to the house in Sean's car. Peter is borrowing it until we head home to Texas. I shift in my seat. When I speak, I don't look at Peter. "Aren't you afraid that I snapped?"

We haven't spoken about what I did to Dean, but the thoughts float through my mind. Peter looks over at me. I feel his gaze on the side of my face. "No, you've been through a lot, Sidney. And piss-poor judgment on his part made him a walking target."

"The things you said to me that night—how did you know what was going through my head?"

Peter doesn't answer right away. He grips the wheel harder and focuses on the road. The ride back from the cemetery is long, and Peter takes a less direct route so we can talk. "I know because I had the same opportunity. The night Gina was killed, I rounded on one of the guys and stabbed him with his own knife. I couldn't stop. I couldn't think. It was instinct. The memory is there in the back of my mind. I can still sense the blade in my hand and feel it tearing through his flesh. It's blinding and overpowers every good deed I ever did. I stopped fighting for her. I changed who I was, but at the depths of my soul I was still the same man. I'd kill again if it would bring her back.

"That's why Sean sent you away. He knew I'd snap if I was pushed too far, since I already had once before. I didn't know what happened. After you left, I asked Sean, but he gave me a story and I believed it. He said you needed some time alone, which seemed off.

"Then Sean told me a bunch of crap about how you demanded money from him—he even showed me your bank account with all the cash he wired. He took a dirty shot. Someone did that to me before, and he knew it'd slow me down. Sean played me. I'm sorry I doubted you. I'm sorry it took me so long to get out here.

"I followed you last night to the grocery store and then to the park. I didn't understand why you went with Dean after you fought like hell last time he tried something. That's why I trailed you, and apparently Sean was following me to make sure I didn't put the guy in the ground.

"So to answer your question, I knew how you'd feel after you stabbed him, because I've done it. I didn't want you to feel like that, ever. I want that ghost gone, but the best I can do is banish him for a while. I love you, Sidney. I wish I could do more. I wish I could make it all go away."

I don't know what to say. "You killed someone?"

Peter nods, and regret flashes across his face. "It was self-defense, but murder is murder. The guy bled out and died on the way to the hospital. He died because of me. No matter what I do, that's always there. That's why I knew what you were thinking that night because I thought the same things myself."

"I didn't take money from Sean. Actually, I told him—"

Peter smiles at me. "I know. He told me on the way here that you said you'd shove any extra cash up his ass. He's kind of a dick like that. I'll beat the shit out him later if it makes you feel better." He's joking, a little bit, maybe.

"At least someone is looking out for you."

"Yeah, I suppose." Peter pulls on to my street and rolls to a stop in front of my parents' house. There are lights on, and I know it's packed with people and food. "Do we have to go in right away?"

Peter shakes his head and cuts the engine. "No, we don't have to. Let's walk around the block. Come on. The fresh air will help."

Peter walks around and plucks me from the car. We start walking, and his phone buzzes. Someone keeps texting him. "Who's that?"

"Jonathan." Peter holds my hand, looking straight ahead as he says it.

"Really? What does he want?"

"Well, he wants me to drive out to this place in Islip and see why Mom wants to kill him. He also wants me to stick around. The nosy kid found out that I'm currently without an employer and has been making outlandish job offers."

"Really?" Peter nods with a slight smile on his face. "What'd you tell him?"

Peter kicks a rock with his saddle shoe. "I told him that I wasn't interested. I want you to take all the time you need with your family. Jon can always find someone else to fix his latest and greatest blunder."

"Peter…" I stop in my tracks and look up at him. "You can't say things like that. You have no job and no money."

He shrugs. "I have enough to get me through this. Besides, it's not like I'd leave you now—you're mine, body, mind, and soul."

I worry about him and it shows on my face. Maybe he is like his younger brother, walking around with his head in the clouds somewhat. People need money to live, and Peter doesn't seem to be in a rush to secure another job. After the way he left the university, I'm not even sure he can be employed somewhere else. I can picture Peter's hands filling out a job application:

REASON LEFT LAST JOB: *Slept with my student.*

Technically, I wasn't Peter's student when he slept with me—unless that's literal and someone is counting sleeping—but looks are just as damning. There were rumors flying around about the two of us long before anything happened. I smirk, thinking back. I had no idea he liked me so much.

Peter squeezes my hand. "What are you thinking about in that beautiful mind of yours?"

"About how we met and that I had no idea things would end up here. I'm glad they did. I wouldn't trade a second of those months away."

Peter lifts my hand to his lips and smiles at me. "Same here. And I'm so glad you finally gave me some *coffee* because I was seriously parched and had no idea. Like none." He's smiling at me. "So what now? Are we headed back to Texas or do we become Jersey folk?" Peter turns and we continue walking, and turn the corner. We're headed back to my house again. I can see the porch light from here along with scads of cars parked up and down the street like a string of army ants.

"Jersey folk? Who talks like that? You're from Long Island—and don't think I didn't notice that whole 'I'm from Connecticut,' you liar, because I noticed. You're supposed to have a Gawd-awful accent in there somewhere, Mr. New Yorker, along with a natural scorn for anything awesome that comes out of Jersey, like me."

"I didn't lie. I came to Texas by way of Connecticut."

"Same difference, fibber."

"Not quite, coffee girl." Peter stops me a few houses away and looks down into my eyes with a sexy smile on his face. "And I notice you dodged my question, which makes me think you haven't decided yet."

"I really don't know what to do." I tuck my hair behind my ear and take a deep breath to steady myself. Emotionally, I feel about as strong as a wet tissue. "I've wasted so much time. I still have one parent and the ugly stepsister back there. It feels like I shouldn't run away this time. Maybe I can fix things or just start over."

"Wait a second. Is the ugly stepsister Mr. Turkey or Sam? Because I can see the title fitting either of them quite well."

"Stop talking trash about Mr. Turkey." Of course I meant Sam. He's such a jerk, but he's still blood. I don't want to write him off again, not without trying to patch things up first. I glance at the house and then back at Peter. "So when did you hear his name?"

"Sam's? You just said it, and I figured it out. Cinderella, ugly stepsister, jealous brother. Got it." Peter taps his index finger against his temple. "You forget how smart I am."

I laugh and swat at him. "Not that! The bird. How'd you know I named him?"

"Oh," Peter takes my hand and starts walking again. "I heard you talking to him when I first found you. It was right before your aunt came out and asked you to go to the store. I wanted to rush up to you and hold you in my arms, but I heard what happened and put the pieces together. Showing up too late was a dick move on my part, and I wasn't sure if you wanted me around. When you gave your dinner to the vulture, you called him Mr. Turkey. I thought it was cute. We should get him a bowtie or something."

"Let's not listen to Sean anymore, like ever, okay?"

"That is the most brilliant idea I've ever heard. Agreed."

CHAPTER 27

Tapping my thumbs swiftly across the screen, I answer the text from Millie and put my phone on the table. Several days have passed, but I haven't headed back yet. Millie did the math and realizes that I'm cutting it really close. I tell her not to worry and put the phone down. I just didn't want to leave Dad yet. He likes having me around. The only time he smiles is when he walks into a room and sees me. There's always surprise on his face, like he'd forgotten that I came back.

Peter glances over at me. Dad's been letting him sleep on the couch, which helps a lot. If I can't sleep, I come downstairs and sit with Peter on the sofa. He wraps his arms around me and we stare at the television until dawn. I manage to pass out for a few hours at a time. I keep reminding myself that time will lessen the vise on my heart, that it'll unclamp eventually and I'll be happy again.

Peter pokes his pancakes. Aunt Beth is still cooking for us. At first I thought she was here for Dad, but I think she's here for her. Mom and my aunt were good friends, and I can tell that my aunt feels better when she's in the kitchen cooking. I'm going to get so fat—well, Mr. Turkey is going to be morbidly obese. The bird eats anything I don't finish, and he really likes bacon. I'm thinking about taking a pound of uncooked bacon out of the package and dropping it off the roof so it splatters on the patio. It'll be like old times for the bird, minus the trucks.

"Stop hording bacon for that beast." Peter reaches across and steals a strip from me.

"There's plenty more bacon, hon!" Aunt Beth calls out from the kitchen.

I grab the strip away just as Peter's about to eat it, and he bites air. I laugh and toss it out the back door to Mr. Turkey. "Get your own."

"You did not just do that," Peter says after blinking in shock. He's got dark, tousled hair, two-day scruff on his beautiful face, and a flick of mirth in his eyes. A dark T-shirt clings to his chest and makes his eyes appear bluer than possible. Without warning, Peter leans into me and tickles my side.

I nearly jump out of my seat, trying to avoid his hands, but Aunt Beth is there. She swats him with the back of the spatula. "None of that at the table, young man."

I laugh because he's a doctor and my aunt is scolding him like a child. It's hysterical, and Peter has no idea what to do with it. He finally swallows his smile and says, "Sorry, ma'am. It won't happen again."

"Ma'am?" Aunt Beth glares at him. "How old do you think I am?"

I point at Peter and laugh. "Come on, Dr. Granz, kiss her ass and say sorry."

He looks confused. That phrase is respectful in Texas, but up here the women act like it means they're old and decrepit. I continue to snigger at him and get a smack with the spatula, too.

Aunt Beth shakes her head at me. "Table manners, Sidney. And stop feeding that thing. It'll never leave if you're giving it bacon every day."

"I'll never leave if you keep feeding me bacon every day," Peter says to Aunt Beth.

It was the right thing to say because she beams. "Oh, stop." Then she takes his plate and says, "Let me get you some more."

Peter waggles his brows after folding his arms across his chest. He leans his chair back so it's on two legs and gives me the most arrogant smirk I've ever seen. "She likes me better than the turkey."

"Everyone likes you better than the turkey."

"What about you?"

"At the moment, or in general?" I don't look at him. I take a bite of muffin, or I plan on it, but Peter swats it out of my hands and the treat lands on my plate.

I do a slow-motion turn and see Peter looking pleased with himself. "You suck."

"You like it."

My jaw drops into a surprised smile and I shove his shoulders. The chair slips out from under him, and Peter topples over onto the floor. Aunt Beth choses that moment to appear in the doorway. "Enough of this. If you two want to act like children, then go outside." She places the bacon on Peter's plate, picks it up, and shoves it in his hand before clapping at us. "Come on. Take your things and eat in the yard. Out!"

Trying to keep from laughing, I grab my plate and walk out the door while biting my tongue. Peter follows after me with a shocked expression on his face. When we're at the swing, he sits next to me and says, "She threw us out."

I start laughing loudly and shove his shoulder. "You are such an ass."

"Sidney, focus on something besides my ass. I think we just pissed your aunt off. She banished us to the yard with the bird." Mr. Turkey chooses that moment to creepily saunter forward, looking for food. I toss him Peter's bacon. "Oh, you did not just do that."

"I believe I did. What you gonna do about it, Professor?" I tilt my head to the side and fold my arms across my chest.

Peter laughs and lunges at me. My plate of food goes flying with half of it landing on me and the rest falling to the ground under the swing. "You suck!"

"So you've said." Peter pushes me back so I'm lying on my back on the swing and he's leaning over me. He doesn't pin my wrists, so I don't freak out. Plus there's egg yolk dripping down my forehead like I've been shot in the head by a chicken. Peter dips his finger in the yellow goo and trails it down to my cheeks and makes a heart.

I squeal, kick, and laugh. I manage to push him off and Peter falls off the swing. I roll and land on top of him. Grabbing the fallen food, I take some scrambled eggs and try to shove them in his mouth—grass and all. "Eat it, Ferro. Come on, open wide."

A horribly wicked grin crosses his face, which makes me go still. "Sidney, please, it's not coffee time yet." He starts laughing so hard that his whole body shakes with me on top.

"Say that again. I dare you."

"Talk dirty to me—" Peter doesn't finish the sentence because I shove the eggs into his mouth. He's grinning at me. Instead of spitting the fallen food out, he chews it and says, "It's a little crunchy."

"Hey!" Dad yells from the back porch. "You get off of him. Don't make me get the hose, Sid!"

My face turns beet red and I slip off of Peter and sit down hard next to him. Peter can't stop grinning. He looks back at my dad and waves. My father shakes his head. "You don't want to be on my list, boy. It ends with a shovel and a long car ride, if you know what I mean. Get her knocked up and I'll ruin your life, kid." Dad walks inside without waiting for an answer.

Peter and I look at each other and we both start laughing like crazy. After a few minutes Peter lies back on the lawn and says, "I didn't knock you up, did I? Just for the record, I need to know that kind of thing so I can buy you and the baby a house and run like hell when your father finds out."

"I'm not pregnant, Peter. I'm on the pill. I've been on it since stuff happened with the asshole." I pull my knees into my chest and wrap my arms around my ankles. "So do you want the 2.5 kids, the little house, and the whole picket-fence thing?"

"Maybe." He grins so hard that I know he's teasing me and means *hell yeah*. "What about you?"

"Maybe. It probably depends on who's knocking me up and buying the house, you know. Little things like that."

"Me." Peter's voice is deadly serious. "What if I was the one who held you at night, every night? What if I was the father of your children? And the surrogate parent of your vulture? What would you think of that?"

I tap my finger to my lip as if I'm pondering the thought. "Would there be dancing?"

He nods. "Always. Would there be bacon?"

I laugh. "Of course. What's the American dream without bacon?"

"You'll have to promise to love me with love handles, because your aunt's cooking and the massive amount of bacon will result in plumpness." Peter tucks his hands behind his head. There isn't anything plump about him, and he eats like the vulture.

"Only if you promise to love me forever and give me a lifetime supply of coffee. It turns out that I really like the *coffee*." I wink at him and can no longer contain my smile. It spreads across my face and seeps inside of me. "The past few days have been so hard and so wonderful, too. I don't want you to go, but I know you have to. Things can't stay this way forever."

"Who says they can't?" Peter looks at the food all over the ground. Mr. Turkey has returned and is pecking a piece of sausage over by the egg and muffin remains. Peter scrambles over to the spilled food, shooing the bird. He lifts the muffin that I tried to eat several times and brushes it off. "I planned this whole romantic thing, but let me ask you this— will you marry me?"

I think he's kidding. I tuck my hair behind my ear and tease him. "You like the coffee, too, admit it."

Peter walks toward me on his knees and hands me the muffin. "I love the coffee. I love you."

I take the muffin and look at it. "What?"

"I know we both can't eat food that fell on the ground, but how about you look for the surprise inside?"

"What are you talking about?" I laugh and look over at him. What did he do? I start pulling the muffin apart until something hard hits my finger. After brushing away the crumbs, I'm left holding a diamond ring between my fingers. I look at the ring and then back up at Peter. "You're really asking me?"

"Yes, I want to spend the rest of my life making you happy. Will you marry me, Sidney?"

My face scrunches into the worst expression I can imagine. Laughter and tears blur together and I bleat like a sheep. Peter smiles uncertainly, waiting for my answer, but I can't speak. I throw my arms around his neck, practically knocking him over, and shake my head. "Yes, yes!"

Peter picks me up and spins me around. We both shriek and laugh until he sets me down. Then Peter hollers at the back door, "She said yes! You can come outside now!"

I glance at him, surprised, and then at the door. My aunt rushes toward us with a weepy smile on her face and the spatula still in hand. She hugs both of us at the same time and is a mess of incoherent babbling.

When we pull away, Daddy is standing there looking stern. "I meant what I said. You take care of her."

"I will, sir." Peter shakes Dad's hand before he turns to me and hugs me so tight that my head pops off.

Sam is behind them, looking Samish. He's pouting today because Dean decided to move on a whim. Like the guy packed up his stuff and fled. When Sam told me that, I was so glad that I had trouble hiding it. There's no chance of seeing Dean again at all. After Sean and Peter finished with him, Dean ran off with his tail between his legs. Dean didn't tell Sam anything, just that he'd had it with this hellhole and had to take off for someplace better.

Sam tries to feign happiness. "Congratulations, Sid. I'm happy for you." He gives me a quick hug and then walks over to Peter. "Don't make me kick your ass if you mistreat her."

I watch to see Peter's reaction and hope he doesn't knock Sam's head off his shoulders. Sam always says the wrong thing and now is no exception. Peter gives my brother a lopsided grin and pulls him into a bear hug like the one my dad just gave me. "Wouldn't think of it, kid. And I'd always wanted a bouncing baby brother like you!" Sam pulls away with a funny look on his face while the rest of us laugh. Sam finally smiles and offers his hand to

Peter. They shake and lean in, saying more things that I can't hear.

"I knew she was after your money, Pete. Why else would she say yes?" I turn quickly on my heel. Sean is standing behind everyone, looking smug. He's got that leather jacket and biker boots, and looks beyond scary with his helmet under one arm. I'm sure my dad is glad that I picked Peter and not Sean.

"Jackass!" Peter says proudly, "You came!" Peter's got his brother in his arms in two seconds. They slap each other on the back and then on the face, like they've done that since they were kids.

"Of course I came. When you said you were giving her a ring, I wanted to make sure she didn't eat it by accident. Who puts a ring in a muffin?" Sean shakes his head in disapproval, like it was a stupid way to propose.

"Are you ever polite?" I ask and fold my arms over my chest, glaring at him.

"Are you seriously asking me that question?" Sean tries to hide a smile as he walks toward me and hands me a little box. "Here."

I glance around. "If Mr. Turkey's heart is in here on a pillow—"

"Just open the box, wiseass." Sean turns away, but the hostile looks he's getting from Dad and Aunt Beth make him turn back again.

I pull away the paper to reveal a little black box. Honestly, I'm afraid to open it. I glance at Peter. "Do you know what it is?" He shakes his head and steps closer.

"People typically find out the answer to that sort of question by removing the lid." Sean's gaze catches mine. His expression is almost daring me to open the box, which totally freaks me out. I look around for my turkey, seriously concerned this time. "For God's sake." Sean reaches forward and lifts the lid. There is a pillow inside the little box. Attached to the pillow is a little bow that's holding a brass key in place.

I untie the bow and lift the key. "What is this?"

"The little house with the white picket fence, minus the two kids, because I'm not doing that with you." Sean's snarky tone makes Peter reach out and smack his brother on the back of the head.

I stare at the key. "You bought us a house?"

"Yeah, I thought you'd like it." I shake my head and try to hand him the key, but Sean steps back, saying, "No returns, Sidney."

"Well." I don't know what to say or what to ask. The gift is way too much and extremely unexpected. I think of a hundred reasons why I can't accept it, but something about the way Sean's standing lets me know how hard this is for him, that he's really trying to patch things up, but he knows that he completely sucks at it. The whole situation is awkward. Sean's been a prick since day one. I don't know what to do with this version of Peter's brother.

I swallow back down the discomfort and ask, "Where is it?"

"Far from here, at least four of five blocks that way." Sean points and the corners of his lips twitch like he wants to laugh. "I heard that second chances are hard to come by and I wanted to make sure that you guys got yours."

"You bought us a house?" Peter finally says, and sounds as shocked as I am.

"Why is everyone looking at me like I'm crazy? Where were you going to live? You needed a house, right?" Sean looks at Aunt Beth for confirmation, expecting her to agree.

Her eyebrows have crept up under her curled hair. She uses a tone that let's Sean know he bought the wrong thing, but she's gentle with him, like he's five years old. "Engagement gifts are usually cookie jars, dear. Something small. A house isn't small."

That makes everyone laugh. Sean smirks and lets the laughter roll off. "Fine, I'll buy them a bigger house for the wedding."

"No, no! One house is plenty." I'm standing in front of Sean, looking up into his face. For a second I think I see what Avery sees when she looks at him, but then the walls shoot up and it's gone. "I thought you didn't like me."

"I never said that," Sean replies.

"Uh, yeah, you did. You said something along the lines of 'I loathe you.'"

He shrugs his shoulders like it doesn't matter. "Yes, well it turns out that I was teasing. You have more backbone than most men, which is something to be admired."

"You admire me?"

"I didn't say that." Sean grins and turns away from us. He speaks over his shoulder as he walks off. "Take care of her, Peter. I'll be in the city for a few more weeks trying to wrap things up and save Jonathan from himself. That kid is going to get disowned at the rate he's going, and I don't want them trying to throw the whole heir thing back my way. Anyway, come visit whenever you want and bring your fiancée."

Sean disappears around the side of the house. After a few moments we hear a motorcycle engine rev as he takes off. Until that point, everyone was staring at each other like Sean was some sort of demented Santa Claus.

I let out a breath. "Well, that was unexpected and a little weird."

"Very. Sean hates everyone, but you won him over." Peter pinches my cheek and laughs as I swat him away. Making nice with Sean is too weird.

"He probably bought us a shack with an outhouse."

Dad speaks up for the first time during this conversation. "Last I checked, there weren't any hobo-style houses over on Sycamore. I think the guy really bought you a house."

Peter takes my hand and presses it to his lips. "Do you want to go see your new house, Future Mrs. Granz?"

"Totally. I need to see it to believe it. If Sean likes me, my whole axis-of-evil theory kind of got fried since Sean was the overlord." It makes me wonder why Sean erected so many barbed walls around himself. It's like he doesn't want anyone to give him a second glance, never mind get close.

The entire family follows us as we drive over to the address on the inside of the box. Sean had it written on the lid of the box in a fancy script. When I opened it, I didn't realize what it was. I thought it was the store where he got the key, not the address of our new house.

When Peter and I stop outside the house, it's so cute that I can't contain my excitement. It's a little Cape Cod, painted gray and white, with a big blue bow on the door. The front yard has been manicured with flower gardens like my mother had. Shasta daisies, impatiens, and big leafy hostas are everywhere. It looks like Sean copied her gardens exactly and put them here. I press my lips together as hard as I can, afraid that I'm going to start crying.

Peter pulls me from the car and walks hand in hand with me up the slate sidewalk to the front door. "The key, Mrs. Granz." I hand it to Peter, and he unlocks the door.

I glance back at the flowers and the fresh paint. "How did he do this so fast?"

Peter shrugs. "It's Sean. How does he do anything?" Peter takes my hand and puts it around his neck before sweeping me off my feet. I yelp as he picks me up.

"What are you doing?"

"Well, this is going to be our house. I have to carry you over the threshold. Or would you prefer to carry me?" Peter grins at me.

"I'll carry you on our wedding day."

"Deal." Peter carries me inside and stops. The house is beautiful and fully furnished. My jaw drops, and there's no way to take it all in fast enough. "Wow." Peter turns slowly, still holding me. There's a new kitchen, decked out with stainless appliances, granite counter tops, and the cutest bistro set I've ever seen. The dark floors from that room flow into the living room where we are standing. There's a fluffy white couch, built-in bookcases, a corner fireplace, and a huge television. My dad grunts with approval and finds a seat on the couch.

Peter turns again and faces a narrow staircase that leads to the bedrooms upstairs. "Want to go check it out?"

"Hell, yes. After seeing this, I want to run up the stairs." Peter sets me down and walks up the staircase with me. There's a small bathroom in the hall and a lovely second bedroom, complete with bed, nightstand, and a comfy chair. "This is so pretty."

Peter cracks the door to the master bedroom and says, "You're going to love this." I walk up behind him and try to peek around, but Peter pulls the door so I can't see. "While I was talking to Sean, I mentioned some things. I didn't tell him to do any of this. He figured it out on his own."

I laugh nervously. "Okay, now you're freaking me out." Peter smiles softly and pushes the door open. I stand frozen in the doorway. "Oh my God, it's beautiful." Everywhere I look is perfect. The room is soft colors, a very pale blue with big fat white moldings. The dark floor is stained with a gloss that's so shiny I can see my reflection. A big bed is against one wall with a padded headboard that has little jewels nestled in the tufts. A downy white bedspread is on top, and sheer fabric flows from the ceiling to the floor, draping the head of the bed. In the corner is an antique record player. I walk toward it slowly, thinking that it's a reproduction of an old Victrola, but when I'm standing over it I do a double take. I point at the record player. "Oh my God! That's real!"

Peter is walking around in the closet— at least I thought it was a closet, but his voice echoes. "Read the record label."

I glance at the black disc and squeal. "It's Benny Goodman! How did he find this stuff?" I turn the player on, careful not to scratch the record, and hear one of my favorite songs. "Oh my God, Peter. Could this be more perfect?"

"I don't know. You haven't seen this room yet." He sticks his head out and says, "Come take a look."

I walk through the small doorway, thinking that it's a storage room or something, and then gape. The attic was converted into a massive master bathroom. A white claw-foot tub sits under a skylight. White cabinets line the walls with big mirrors centered above hammered copper sinks. Tiny pale blue glass tiles glitter within wall niches, and a beautiful huge shower is nestled into the corner of the room. I stand there, staring.

"How did he have time to do this?"

Peter walks up behind me and wraps his arms around my waist. "The obvious answer is that he started this the night he met you, but that seems unbelievable based on the way he behaved."

"Just a bit, yeah."

"I told him that I wanted to marry you, that you were the one. He knew from that night forward that I was serious about you." Peter turns me around in his arms. "This is a helluva present."

I nod and smile. "It means I don't have to leave Dad, and that me and you can have a fresh start, but what about a job?"

Peter releases me and pulls his phone from his back pocket. He taps the screen as he talks. "Since we'll be sharing a bank account, you should know our financial situation. Here"—he hands me his phone—"take a look."

I take it and glance down at the screen. I blink a few times, thinking that I'm seeing it wrong. When I glance up, Peter is smiling. "You said you were broke." I don't understand. He's loaded. Peter doesn't have to work if he doesn't want to, like ever. There's more money in his account than what Sean offered me back at the Ferro mansion.

"I said I wasn't the heir and that I was all right, and I am. I invested my trust fund and did well. I lived off my salary so this kept growing. I'm not as rich as Sean or Jon, but I'm far from broke." Peter grins at me. "I told you that I'd take care of you. Did you really think I had nothing?"

I nod and shove my eyeballs back into my face. "Well, yeah. Your living room was full of flakeboard furniture. It looked more like a dorm room than a professor's home."

He shrugs. "It wasn't home to me, so I didn't spend much to fix it up. There was no reason to, not until I met you."

"So you don't have to work?" Peter shakes his head. "But I bet you want to teach."

He nods and steps toward me. "Yeah, I liked being in a classroom."

"We'll have to do something about that."

"Actually," Peter says and glances up at me from under those dark lashes, "I already have. Remember how I mentioned that Jon's impulsive? Well, he bought something around here a couple years back."

"What did he buy?"

"A private school. He was trying to impress a hot girl."

"Aren't we all?" I can't imagine how that would help Jon impress a girl, but it sounds about right based on what Sean and Peter said about the youngest Ferro.

Peter laughs and says, "Jonathan Ferro Prep is about an hour from here and needs an English teacher."

"Is that so, Professor?"

He nods. "After my mother stormed off, Jon said he'd make me king if I helped him deal with Mom and his latest investment. When I realized where this school was located, I said yes. The only hitch in my devious master plan was if you wanted to go back to Texas or you said no when I proposed. I totally thought the turkey was going to eat your ring, by the way…speaking of the fat bird, come here." Peter moves to the window and pulls back the curtain. "Check it out."

I glance down and see an enormous perch right next to the patio with a big black bird sitting on it. "Aw, Sean delivered Mr. Turkey after we left."

"So"—Peter turns me toward him—"are we staying here or moving back to Texas?"

"It sounds like it's time to start over and this is the perfect place, the perfect house, with the perfect husband-to-be."

Peter takes me in his arms and dips his head, pressing his lips to mine. When he pulls away, he says, "I love you, Sidney Colleli."

"I love you, too, Peter Granz. Now give me some of that coffee you're always talking about."

AUTHOR'S NOTE

Thank you to all the amazing fans who love Peter (Ferro) Granz and Sidney! You guys rocked DAMAGED 1 onto the best-seller lists where it stayed for a crazy long time!

If you love Peter, you should check out two more series with the other Ferro Brothers: THE ARRANGEMENT revolves around the dangerous and devastated Sean Ferro, and STRIPPED is a novel that tells the story of the youngest Ferro brother, Jonathan.

These three series crisscross at points giving you more of the characters you love!

THE ARRANGEMENT
(Sean Ferro's Story)

STRIPPED
(Jonathan Ferro's Story)
A Novel

To ensure you don't miss any of the
FERRO brothers, text
AWESOMEBOOKS to **22828** and you
will get an e-mail reminder on release day,
and pre-order STRIPPED today.

TURN THE PAGE
To see how Sean Ferro and Avery met
in *New York Times* bestselling series
THE ARRANGEMENT

THE ARRANGEMENT

VOL. 1

BY

H.M. WARD

CHAPTER 1

The night air is frigid. It doesn't help that I'm stuck wearing this little black dress in my crap car. I shiver as I try to keep the engine running at a red light. My little battered car is from two decades ago and stalls if I don't rev the engine while I have my foot on the brake. I'm driving with two feet in a car that's supposed to be an automatic. The heater doesn't work. If I try to turn it on, I'll get my face blasted with white smoke. It's awesome, in an utterly humbling kind of way. At least the car is mine. It gets me where I need to go, most of the time.

The light flips to green and I botch it. I don't gas the car enough, and it shudders and stalls. I grumble and grab for the can of ether. The cars behind me blare their horns.

I ignore them. They can go around me. I grab the can on the seat next to me, kick open my door, and walk around to the hood. I shake the can and spray it into the engine intake. The car will start up as soon as I turn the key now, and I can drive away in shame.

The night air is crisp and filled with exhaust. This road is always busy. It doesn't matter what time of day it is. Angry drivers move around me. Everyone is always in a hurry. It's part of the New York frame of mind. I'm treated to a catcall as a car full of guys blows past me. I flip them the bird and hear their laughter echo as they fade from sight.

Tonight couldn't possibly get any worse. I put the cap on the can of ether. Then it happens. My night takes a one-eighty straight into suckage.

As I drop the hood, it slams shut, and I look through the windshield.

"Seriously?" I say at the guy who jumps in my seat. He's wearing a once-blue fluffy coat and hasn't shaved for weeks. He turns the key and my crappy car roars to life. He gasses it and takes off, swerving around me. I stand in the lane staring after him. What a moron. Who'd steal that piece of trash?

Still, it's my car and I need it. After the night I had, I don't want to run after him, but I have to. I need that car. I take off at a full run. My lungs start to burn as I suck in frozen air and exhaust. I run down the shoulder, avoiding trash that's lying in the gutter. My attention is singularly focused on my car. I push my body harder and feel my muscles protest, but I don't hold back. He's getting away.

I manage to run a block when a guy on a motorcycle slows next to me. "That guy stole your car." He sounds shocked.

I can't see his face through the black helmet. It has a tinted visor that covers his face. "No shit, Sherlock," I huff and keep running. My purse is in the car, my only pair of work-acceptable heels, my books— aw, fuck, my books. I paid over a grand for those. They're worth more than the car. I run faster. My dress flares around my thighs as my Chucks help me sprint forward. My body doesn't want to do it. The stitch in my side feels like it's going to bust open.

The guy on the bike is annoying. He rolls next to me and flips up his face shield. I glance at him, wondering what he's doing. Biker guy looks at me like I'm crazy. "Are you trying to catch him?"

"Yes." Pointing ahead, huffing. There are three lights on this stretch of road before the ramp to get on the parkway. If he hits a red light, the car will stall and I'll get it back. My lungs are burning, and it's not like I have time to explain this. My car has already passed the first light. "If he stops, the car will stall."

"You want me to help?" He glances at the car and then back at me.

I stop and nearly double over. Holy hell, I'm out of shape. I nod and throw my leg over the back of his bike, flashing the cars driving past us. I so don't care. Wrapping my arms around his waist, I hold on tight and say, "Go."

"I was going to call the cops, but this works, too." He sounds amused. I hold onto his trim waist and plaster myself against his back. He's wearing a leather jacket, and I can feel his toned body through the supple material. He pulls into traffic and zips through the lanes. The wind blasts my hair and plasters my eyelashes wide open. We bob and weave, getting closer and closer to my car. My heart is racing so fast that it's going to explode.

I see my car. It's passing the second light. Motorcycle man punches it, and the bike flies under the second intersection just as the light changes. I manage not to shriek. My skirt flies up to my hips, but I don't let go of the biker's waist to push the fabric back down.

We're nearly there when the thief catches the third light. The car in front of him stops, forcing the carjacker to stop as well. As soon as he takes his foot off the gas, my car convulses and white smoke shoots out the tailpipe. The engine ceases. The driver's side door is kicked open and the guy runs.

Motorcycle man pulls up next to my car. I slip off the back of the bike, my heart beating a mile a minute. I can't afford to lose this stuff. I'm barely making it as it is. I look at my car. Everything is still there. I turn back to the guy on the bike as I smooth my skirt back into place.

Tucking my hair behind my ear, I say, "Thanks." I must seem insane.

He flips his face shield up and says, "No problem. Does your car always do that?" A pair of blue eyes meets mine, and the floor of my stomach gives way. Damn, he's cute. No, not cute—he's hot.

"Get jacked? No, not always."

He smiles. There's a dusting of stubble on his cheeks. I can barely see it because of the helmet. He raises an eyebrow at me and asks, "This has happened before, hasn't it?"

More times than you'd think. Criminals are really stupid. "Let's just say this isn't the first time I had to chase after the car. So far no one's made it to the parkway. That damn light takes forever and I keep stalling out in the same spot. You'd think I'd figure it out by now, but…" But I'm mentally challenged and prefer to chase after car thieves. I stop talking and press my lips together. His eyes run over my dress and pause on my sneakers, before returning to my face. Great, he thinks I'm mental.

Turning to the car, I grab another can of ether from the backseat and walk around to the front. I dropped the last can somewhere behind me. I pop the hood and spray. I'm so cold that I've gone numb. As I walk back to my door, I shake my head, saying, "Who steals a car that barely runs?"

"Do you need any help?" The guy holds my gaze for a moment, and my stomach twists. He seems sincere, which kills me. A strange compulsion to spill my guts tries to overtake me, but I bash it back down.

Pressing my lips together, I shake my head and swallow the lump in my throat. Today sucked. I'm totally alone. No one helps me, and yet this guy did. "No, I'm okay," I lie as I slip into my car and yank the door shut. "Thanks for the ride." I turn the engine over and smile at him. The window is down. It doesn't go up.

"Anytime." He nods at me, like he wants to say something else. All I can see of his face is his crystal blue eyes and a beautiful mouth. He's sitting on a bike that cost more than my tuition. He's loaded, and I've got nothing. A pang of remorse shoots through me, but I need to go. The haves and the have-nots weren't made to mingle. I already learned that lesson once. I don't need to learn it again.

"Thanks," I say before he can ask my name. "I'll see you around." I smile at him and drive away, holding back tears that are building behind my eyes.

It's weird. There are so many shitty people in the world, and on the worst day of my life, I finally find a nice one and I'm driving away from him.

THE ARRANGEMENT

Volumes are on sale now and follow the story of SEAN FERRO

MORE ROMANCE BOOKS BY H.M. WARD

THE ARRANGEMENT

SCANDALOUS

SCANDALOUS 2

SECRETS

THE SECRET LIFE OF TRYSTAN SCOTT

And more.

To see a full book list, please visit:
www.SexyAwesomeBooks.com/books.htm

CAN'T WAIT FOR H.M WARD'S NEXT STEAMY BOOK?

Let her know by leaving stars and telling her what you liked about DAMAGED 2 in a review!

CPSIA information can be obtained at www.ICGtesting.com
Printed in the USA
LVOW11s0547100115

422247LV00001B/8/P

9 780615 826813